SELCOUTH

SELCOUTH

T.J. Walker

Charleston, SC
www.PalmettoPublishing.com

Paperback ISBN: 979-8-8229-3973-8

Selcouth

(adj.) unfamiliar, rare, strange, and yet marvelous

Pronunciation: sel-'kooth

PART ONE

Abditory

(n.) a place into which you can disappear;
a hiding place

I

Heavy footsteps ran through the underbrush. Dead leaves crunched loudly underfoot. Fallen branches reached out, grabbing hold of clothing that clung to sweat-soaked skin. Her breathing was labored as she ran, her chest burning with every inhale. Ducking behind a tree, she stopped dead in her tracks. With both hands on her chest, she tried her hardest to quiet herself and listen to her surroundings.

The air was full of chirping crickets and the occasional rustling of leaves. The unmistakable sound of footsteps came from her left, and she held her breath. At a distance much closer than she'd have liked, she could see the beams of flashlights panning the horizon between the trees. She started to run. She heard her pursuers starting to shout in muffled voices and knew that her sudden movement had startled them. She never looked behind her as she ran. She didn't want to be disappointed if she were to look back and see their lights getting brighter as they gained on her.

She hadn't been running again for long when her foot caught on a raised root and sent her plummeting to the ground. She barely kept an anguished cry down as she tried to quickly and gently free her ankle. She could already feel it starting to swell, and she prayed to whoever might be listening that it wasn't broken. She looked around her wearily. The only light around her was the pale moonbeams that shone down through the trees, and unless she were sitting directly under one, no one would be able to see her in the brush. The knot in her stomach loosened some when she realized that she no longer heard any distant voices or saw any bobbing flashlights.

Her ankle throbbed. She knew that any more travel tonight would be slow, if any happened at all. Closing her eyes, she hovered her shaking right hand over her injury and tried to concentrate. A very faint white glow illuminated her palm, and she could feel the muscles in her ankle starting to tingle. But all too quickly her heartbeat quickened, her vision got blurry, and she had to stop.

Damn it, she thought as fresh sweat formed on her brow. *The serums from the Lab haven't worn off enough yet.*

She was going to have to stop here, she decided. There wasn't going to be any more walking tonight, let alone running. She tried to gather as big a pile of leaves as she could without venturing from where she sat and formed the pile into a makeshift bed. She got as comfortable as she could, and it wasn't long before she was asleep.

She didn't realize how bad her injury was until the morning. With the help of early morning sunlight coming down through the trees, she examined the very large purple bruise that wrapped around the entirety of her ankle. Some of it even spread down her foot, which was also very swollen.

Something's definitely broken, she thought sadly. She looked around for anything that she could use as a crutch. A few feet to her left she saw a dead branch on the forest floor. She slowly maneuvered herself onto her stomach from her sitting position and proceeded to shimmy her way across the leaf ridden ground toward the stick. When she got to it, she was relieved to discover how sturdy it was. Carefully she got up on her good leg and wedged the branch up under her right arm. She took a few test steps in one direction, and then another in the other. Her ankle hurt like hell, but this was going to have to do.

She hobbled for a mile and a half before anything made her put her guard up again. The distant sound of a truck driving along a gravel road made her stop and crouch low to the ground. Panic formed in her stomach, and her heart started to race.

They've already caught up to me!

She waited in that crouched position until she no longer heard any noises from the passing vehicle. Her good leg was starting to cramp from carrying most of her weight. She sat on a nearby fallen tree and tried to massage out the knots that were forming. After a while of rubbing, her arms were sore, and she just wanted to sit there and rest for a while. Remembering the truck, she knew she couldn't stay stationary long. She tucked the branch up under her arm as she stood and started off in the opposite direction, sending her even farther into the forest.

Her throat was dry, and she'd give just about anything for a drink of water. As she limped along, she tried to stay in the shade as much as she could.

A sudden scattering of leaves startled the girl, and she almost fell backward onto her butt as her head shot up to see what had started to run. Just ahead, a lone deer darted through the trees away from her. Her dirt-caked hands clutched at her chest. She closed her eyes and tried taking deep breaths.

It was just a deer, she thought. *I must have scared it as bad as it scared me.*

A loud *bang* suddenly filled the air.

The barrel of the rifle was the first thing to come out from behind the tree. It was slowly followed by hands, then arms, and finally the whole body of a man. He wore a red long-sleeved checkered shirt, blue jeans, a baseball cap, and heavy-duty boots. He took a few steps out from behind the tree before finally noticing her. And she wasn't hard to see. Against the many shades of green and brown, her bright (not so bright anymore, now that they were caked in dirt) white pants and shirt made it very hard to blend in during the day.

Who the hell is this girl? Bennett wondered as he stared at her, in her tattered hospital-like clothes and makeshift crutch, with a look of pure puzzlement. *Where did she come from? How did she get here?* And he was startled to see the look of terror on her face. Her eyes were as big as dinner plates as she stared at him. Had the gun scared her that bad? *What the hell is going on?*

The man slowly lowered the gun to the ground.

"Hey," he said softly. "Are you all right? What are you doing all the way out here?" He took a small step toward her, and she immediately started to panic, taking many sloppy, hurried steps backward, eventually tripping over the crutch under her arm, landing with a thud. Her face contorted into a grimace as her hands gingerly went to the ankle that the man could now see was very purple and very swollen. He took another step toward her. In a blink, she had the big stick up off the ground and pointed at him. He raised his hands slightly in defense and stopped moving.

"It's ok," he said, trying to soothe her. "You're all right." She was breathing heavily and never took her eyes off him. The man lowered his arms and took a small step back. The stick wavered slightly.

Has she run away from home? Nah, that couldn't be it. There weren't any other houses but his around for at least twenty miles. *And what the hell is she wearing*? he wondered. He knew he wasn't as young as he used to be, but he knew fashion hadn't taken this drastic a turn. The thought that they reminded him of hospital clothes—or something like that—made his heart race a little. Because there wasn't anything like that anywhere near here either. This girl might be in serious trouble.

Slowly, he crouched down, so he wasn't towering over her any longer. "Are you hurt?" he asked softly, feeling a little stupid upon remembering what she had been using the large stick for. "Do you know where you are?" he asked. A few moments went by in silence, with the two staring at the other, before she finally shook her head "no."

"What's your name?" he ventured. Her eyes darted around the woods behind him. She was listening for anything that might be approaching from behind her.

For all she knew, this man was part of the team that was driving her away from the Lab. The man grunted as he sat down on the ground. The crouching was really starting to hurt his knees. He noticed how paranoid she was and sighed to himself. *Poor kid.*

"Well," he started, causing her to look at him again. "My name is Bennett." He grinned. There was something sincere in that smile. A sincerity that made the girl slowly put down the stick that she still had pointed at him. She didn't think that he was a threat. Yet.

"Jade," she finally said, just above a whisper. "My name is Jade."

Jade sat very close to the door inside the truck. Every bump in the road had her banging her shoulder against the frame.

How Bennett had managed to convince her to come with him, he didn't know.

A small cabin suddenly appeared within the trees. Lichen covered the roof in patches of green and gray. A thin plume of smoke drifted up from the chimney. Jade's breath caught in her throat when she saw a figure on the porch. It was another man. He sat, legs propped up ahead of him, on a large porch swing. He was wearing a baggy pair of dark jeans and an even baggier dark gray crew-neck sweatshirt. In his lap lay a book. Mindlessly, his fingers scratched the short beard on his face.

Bennett could feel the anxiety seeping from the girl beside him. He turned off the engine and shifted to face her.

"It'll be all right," he said softly, trying not to spook her. "He's not gonna hurt you. Lewis wouldn't hurt a fly." He finished with a smile. Jade tried her best to smile back at him, but it was obviously forced. She couldn't really trust anyone. Not yet anyway.

Bennett got out of the truck and went around to the other side to help Jade. She hesitated before grabbing his offered arm and carefully stepped down. He handed her the stick that he'd stashed in the truck bed. It was at this time that Lewis finally looked up from his book. He was expecting to see his husband walking up the gravel driveway, rifle slung over his shoulder by the strap, with that big goofy grin that he always wore to meet him. He just assumed Bennett would be alone, like always.

Lewis stared at the two walking (one walking and the other sort of hobbling) up the path toward the house. Slowly getting up off the swing and leaving his book behind, he walked to the steps that led up to the porch. He didn't say anything, just kind of raised his eyebrow at Bennett, who responded with an *I'll tell you in a minute* sort of look.

Bennett helped Jade up the stairs and onto the porch while Lewis held the front door of the cabin open for them. Jade entered first, warily. She hadn't realized how cold it had been outside until she felt the warmth of the fire that was burning across the room. The house smelled like cinnamon, and there were trinkets and books almost everywhere she looked. Pictures and paintings covered the walls. As Jade marveled, Lewis pulled Bennett close to him.

"So, are you going to tell me why you came home with a random girl, Benny?" he questioned just above a whisper. Bennett sighed and looked from Jade to the man beside him.

"I found her in the woods," he started, his eyebrows scrunching together. "I was tracking a deer one minute, and the next she was just standing there, leaning on that big stick and wearing those weird clothes." He looked back to where the girl stood, looking down at a photo of the couple that sat on a small table in between two big reclining chairs. "I think she's running from something. Or some*one*, I guess. She was really spooked."

Lewis looked at the strange girl and then back at Bennett worriedly.

"Well, what if she *is* running from someone? They could come across here looking for her. Who knows what kind of trouble she might be in?" Bennett sighed.

"I thought about that too," Bennett admitted. "But I would have felt too bad about leaving her out there all by herself. I mean, she is hurt after all. What if I'd left her and she died out there?" he asked.

Lewis smiled at him softly, placing a hand on his cheek. "Always too soft for your own good." They both chuckled lightly.

"I guess I should go ahead and call the police, you think?" Bennett asked in a low voice. Lewis nodded, and Bennett made his way to the nearby kitchen counter.

He had only enough time to press one number before the phone was gone. He felt it leave his fingers, as if someone had come and yanked it away. But he didn't see it leave. It was too fast.

The smacking sound of the phone hitting a palm made both men turn their heads. Now facing them, on the other side of the room, Jade stood, one hand holding the makeshift crutch under her arm, the other holding the phone.

"No," she said simply. "I can't let you do that."

II

The two men stood dumbfounded. Lewis was taking slow steps backward toward where Bennett stood, unable to move.

What did I bring into our house? he couldn't help but wonder in horror. He felt strangely ashamed of the thought the moment it came.

Jade stood still, watching the two men's faces. The terror there told her that there was no way they could have had any prior knowledge about her. It really was just a coincidence that Bennett found her when and where he did. Lewis finally reached Bennett and grabbed his arm firmly. His eyes never left the girl in their living room.

"That's all right," Lewis finally managed to say, surprising himself by how steady his voice sounded. His whole body trembled. He wasn't sure who he was trying to convince with that statement. Was it her, and he was saying it was all right to keep the cops out of it? Or was he trying to convince himself that it was all right that this girl just made a phone move—no, *fly*—across the room without touching it?

Jade placed the phone down on the small table at her side. She sighed to herself, a bit relieved—both for the fact that these two men weren't working with the Lab and that those damn serums were fully wearing off. She wanted to try fixing her ankle again but didn't think it would work. She was already feeling slightly dizzy from just moving the phone. She looked to the two terrified men.

"I could really use your help," she said quickly. "But I would understand if you would rather not. And I can't promise people won't come looking for me." She paused. "Dangerous people."

Both men looked at each other for a few moments. They turned back to her.

"Would—" Bennett started, his voice catching. He cleared his throat. "Do you think we could—I mean—"

"Could we talk privately for a moment?" Lewis spewed, knowing that's where Bennett was trying to go. "Just the two of us? Just for a minute?"

A small knot formed in Jade's stomach, but she didn't think they were going to try anything silly. Or stupid. She nodded.

Lewis, who to this point still had a firm grip on the other man's arm, dragged his husband into the nearest room with a door. It happened to be the spare bathroom. They stood silently, staring at each other in the small space.

"What the *fuck*." Lewis finally whispered harshly. Bennett closed his eyes and dragged his hands down his face. He shook his head.

"I—"

"No seriously," Lewis interrupted. "*What the fuck!*"

"I know!" Bennett agreed. He sighed and shuffled over to the toilet and sat on the lid. "What do we do?" he asked, suddenly picking at the skin on his hands. Lewis shrugged roughly, shaking his head.

"I don't even know what to think," he admitted.

"Neither do I."

Both men went silent, thinking.

"I think—" Bennett started, pausing like he was still unsure of what he was about to say. "I think we should help her." He blurted. Lewis's eyes widened. "I think we should *try*, at least." Bennett said quickly, before the other could speak. "I mean, she doesn't have anyone else, L."

Lewis crossed his arms over his chest. "We don't know that," he muttered. Bennett cocked his head.

"I found her in the middle of the woods in the middle of nowhere!"

Lewis sighed and started pacing in the small space. "She said there were going to be people looking for her," he said, biting his nails as he paced.

"All the more reason to help her!" Bennett exclaimed. "She could be in serious trouble! They might be trying to kill her!"

"Exactly!" Lewis shouted, a little too loud for the small space. "What makes you think they wouldn't dispose of us if we tried to keep her from them? Huh? They—whoever the hell 'they' are—probably wouldn't think twice about any civilian casualties! Especially if they're after someone like *her*!" he said, pointing at the thin door that led back to Jade.

In the living room, Jade could hear their muffled voices. The knot in her stomach tightened. Her ankle throbbed. She looked behind her at the reclining chairs and decided to shuffle around and sit in one. She sank more than she thought she would, but boy, was it comfortable. Much more comfortable than the forest floor had been. Even more still than the rickety thing they dared call a bed in the Lab. She suddenly had trouble keeping her eyes open.

"I know you're worried," Bennett began, standing from his seat and grabbing Lewis's hands, stopping his pacing. Lewis scoffed but wouldn't meet his eyes.

"Of course I am." he sighed. "What if something happened? What if something happened to *you*? Who would I have then?" Bennett smiled sadly at Lewis before taking his face in his hands and kissing him softly.

"I'm not goin' anywhere," he assured him, putting their foreheads together. "You're stuck with me, baby." They both laughed lightly.

"Then why do I feel like we're in one of those stories where one of us dies and leaves the other to be the sad lonely old gay guy for the rest of his life?" Lewis groaned, causing them both to laugh again.

"Because it's scary," Bennett admitted, leaning back slightly so he could look at the man in front of him. "This is some shit we have never seen before. But I have faith in our writers that we will make it to the end of this story!" he concluded jokingly. Lewis rolled his eyes and pushed Bennett playfully. They both sighed.

"So, we're doing this then, huh?" Lewis ventured. "We're gonna try to help her, Benny?" Bennett nodded.

"Ok then." Lewis stood up straighter and took a deep breath. "I guess we've kept her waiting long enough." Bennett nodded again.

They were both concerned to not see Jade standing where they left her, but it didn't take long to find her asleep in Lewis's recliner. They both released the breaths they hadn't realized they'd been holding. Lewis started biting his nails again, and Bennett came over and put an arm around his shoulder.

"It'll be all right," he said, trying to reassure him. Lewis nodded, and Bennett gave him a squeeze.

"I guess I'd better go and get that spare room cleaned up, huh?" Bennett suggested, letting his arm fall. "She's gonna need to sleep somewhere other than in our living room."

"Yeah," Lewis agreed. "Good idea."

Bennett disappeared down the hall.

There was a knock at the front door.

III

Lewis's heart was pounding as he walked the few steps it took to reach the front door. *So it's starting already then?* he thought as his hand closed around the handle. He breathed deep and let the breath out slowly before opening the door.

Standing on the porch were two men wearing dark gray suits. The one closest to the door smiled and removed dark sunglasses from his face. The other stood motionless.

"Good morning," the smiling man greeted him. "I'm Officer White. And this is my partner, Officer O'Riley," he said, gesturing to the other man, who merely nodded his head curtly. Lewis leaned on the door, which was open only enough for the officers to see him and nothing else.

"Good morning, officers." He could hear his heartbeat in his ears now. "What can I do for you gentlemen?"

Officer White's eyes darted around the porch momentarily before they landed back on Lewis. "Well, you see, our department is in the process of tracking down a missing person," he began, turning the sunglasses over in his hands. "She's about twenty years old, about yea high, brown hair, brown eyes, and about a hundred and seventy pounds." Lewis couldn't help but notice that O'Riley was slowly turning his head in every direction, searching.

"Have you seen anyone that may fit that description lately?" Officer White asked, gaining Lewis's attention again. Lewis shook his head.

"No. Honestly nobody ever comes out this way," he said, not completely lying. People hardly ever came out this deep into the woods. That's why he and Bennett had moved here. It was their own little oasis. Officer White nodded, and Lewis caught the man's eyes trying to dart into the house. They quickly came back.

"Well," White began, reaching into his jacket pocket. He pulled out a little white card and handed it over. "You give us a call if you see anything then, ok?"

Lewis nodded and took the card. "Sure thing."

Officer White bid him farewell, and the two walked off the porch and back to the black SUV that waited idling on the gravel driveway behind Bennett's truck.

Lewis shut the door and leaned his back against it hard. He stood like that with his eyes closed for a solid minute. He was trying to get his heart to calm down. And it only did when he could finally hear the officers' car retreating down the gravel drive. He opened his eyes and saw Jade staring at him from where she sat in the recliner.

"All right," Bennett's voice called as he came back up the hall. "I think that should be fine for now." The smile he had on his face faded quickly when he saw Lewis. His stride quickened.

"Hey, are you all right?" he asked, worry clear in his voice. "You're white as a sheet." He put a hand to his husband's forehead as he reached him.

Lewis shooed Bennett's hand away. "I'm fine," he grumbled. "It's just that two officers just knocked at our door asking if I'd seen a missing young woman!"

Bennett's face fell even more. Lewis could see fear building in his eyes.

"Did—" he started. "Did they seem...suspicious?"

Lewis rolled his eyes. "Of course they were suspicious," he said . "That's their job, Benny."

"Do you think they'll come back?"

Lewis sighed and shook his head. "I don't know," he admitted. "One of them gave me a business card and told me to call if I saw anything."

It was Bennett's turn to sigh. "Ok," he replied, clearly deep in thought.

Lewis looked back toward Jade, who still sat staring at the pair. Outside, she looked calm, like this was the beginning of any other Thursday.

But inside? Inside, she was petrified. Her insides felt like they were vibrating; her heart felt like it was mere beats away from exploding. She looked down at her hands and started chewing on the inside of her cheek.

I'm going to get them killed, aren't I?

IV

Jade stood at the end of the queen-size bed, staring at the small pile of clothes that Bennett left for her. Water dripped from her hair onto the hardwood floor. Beyond closed curtains, the sky was getting dark.

She carefully felt the fabric of the sweatpants and the big T-shirt. She hadn't had clothes like these in a very, very long time. She put them on, making sure to carefully maneuver around her injured ankle. She had to tie the strings of the pants and roll up the legs because they were *just* too big.

She sat herself on the edge of the bed and propped up her injured leg. She hesitated before hovering a hand over her purple ankle. The tingle started in her foot, and the white glow emanated from her palm. The throbbing got worse momentarily before it finally started to subside. She could feel the muscles tightening one second and going limp the next. A jolt of pain up her leg and a popping sound made her flinch, and she almost lost her concentration. All too quickly her head started to spin, and her heartbeat quickened. She stopped, closing her eyes. She took a deep breath and rotated her ankle slowly.

No pain. Only the slight ache from the bruise that would take a little longer to disappear. She sighed, relieved.

There was a soft tapping at the door, and she jumped.

"Jade?" Bennett's voice called from the other side. "You doin' all right in there?"

Jade panicked, like a child who's done something wrong and is about to get caught. She scrambled for words.

"Yes!" she replied a little too loudly. She cursed herself internally for it. "I'm ok."

"All right," Bennett started again. He felt very unsure of himself and what to do. Should he leave her alone? "Well, Lewis and I have just finished making dinner, if you're up to eating," he said, more as a question than anything else.

Jade sat quietly for a moment until her stomach growled. She really was hungry. She hadn't eaten anything since the day before those trucks took her away from the Lab. "I'll be out in a minute!" she called.

On the other side of the door, Bennett smiled a little, relieved. He retreated down the hall toward the kitchen.

"Is she coming?" Lewis asked from where he was filling his and Bennett's plates at the stove. A small radio on the counter played soft music. An extra plate was sitting, waiting, on the counter beside it.

Bennett nodded, still smiling a little.

The meal had been eaten in silence, with nothing but the radio playing, until all three had finished. And it hadn't been an uncomfortable silence—no one really seemed to notice.

"So," Bennett started, glancing at Lewis for a long moment where he sat before fixing his gaze on Jade. "Can I ask you some questions that might be a bit... personal?" he asked, absentmindedly picking at the skin on his hands.

A knot formed in Jade's stomach. She nodded.

Bennett nodded back slowly, mustering up the courage to ask what he wanted to ask. Lewis placed a reassuring hand on his husband's knee under the table and gave it a little squeeze. *I'm right here if you need me*, the gesture said.

"Well, first I guess I—well, really *we*—wanted to ask about the whole...telekinesis...thing," he said shyly.

Jade flinched slightly at the word, and she hoped they didn't notice.

They did, of course.

"But if it's a sensitive subject, that's totally fine," Lewis jumped in. "You don't have to tell us anything about it now."

Jade nodded. She appreciated that. But she knew she owed them an explanation for it all, especially because they were putting their lives on the line for her, a *stranger*. But it was hard to think about. It *hurt*.

"Would it be easier for you if we continued this conversation in the morning, maybe?" Lewis prompted. "After you've had some sleep?"

Jade looked between the two men. She could see curiosity clearly in their faces. But she also saw concern there. *Genuine* concern. She nodded.

V

"We have something new for you today," said the man approaching the chair. In his hands he held a large syringe filled with a milky-white substance.

"What does it do?" the girl strapped to the chair asked, her voice just above a whisper. Without warning, the long needle sank into the skin just above her collarbone. It ached as the needle dug in, quickly turning cold as the serum was administered. The man took it out with a yank and shrugged.

"Don't know yet. That's why you're here." And with that, he left her alone in the room.

The girl's heart started to race. Whether it was from the serum or anxiety, she couldn't tell. Her head started to throb, her teeth ached, and her vision started to blur around the edges.

She closed her eyes and tried to raise her hands to her head, but they were stopped by the leather straps that held them down. This only made her panic more, which made her head hurt more, and she started thrashing around in the chair. She tried freeing her arms and kicking her legs but failed against the restraints.

A shooting pain in her head had her gritting her teeth and squeezing her eyes shut even tighter. Her heart felt like a hornet's nest inside her chest. It was starting to get harder to breathe, but she couldn't get her body to stop moving.

A scream suddenly filled the air, and it took her a few moments to realize that it was coming from her. She *was the one screaming. And she couldn't get that to stop either.*

Before she knew it, the lights above her head were flickering wildly.

The chair was lifting off the ground.

Jade sat up suddenly. Her heart was racing, and she was struggling to take deep breaths. She fumbled to get the comforter off herself and pulled her knees up to her chest. She was already starting to forget the dream. But not the feeling of it. Never that. That always lingered like a bitter taste in her mouth.

Upon waking and finally coming down from her panic attack, she realized just how dry her throat was. She remembered the glass Bennett had given her before she'd retired to the guest room for the night, and she reached for it where it sat on the little bedside table. She downed the water in three large gulps only to still be thirsty afterward. She looked toward the door.

Would it be fine if I went out there for more? She wondered. *Am I going to wake them up if I do?*

Stealthily, she put her feet to the wood floor and walked across the room. She stood silently for a few moments, with her hand on the door handle, listening. Silently, she turned the knob and pulled the door open. Still no sound. She tiptoed down the hall to the kitchen and stopped in front of the sink. She stood silently for another moment before carefully lifting the handle and allowing a small stream of water to flow into her glass.

She had three full glasses drunk before she heard a small sound behind her and the kitchen light turned on. Her whole body jumped, and she almost dropped the glass in her hand. She quickly turned, and standing just inside the kitchen was Lewis. His hair was a mess, and he was rubbing his eyes with balled-up fists. He finally saw her standing by the sink, staring at him with wide eyes.

"Oh," was all that his half-asleep mind could come up with.

Jade's eyes darted around aimlessly for a moment before she placed the glass on the counter beside her. "I'm sorry," she said quickly, fidgeting with her fingers. "I didn't mean to wake you."

Lewis's eyebrows furrowed and he waved at her dismissively as he started walking toward the other end of the kitchen. "No, no, you're fine," he said, his voice groggy. "I wake up in the middle of the night a lot."

Jade nodded, and she watched him open a cabinet and pull out a small jar of what looked like little gummies. He took two out and popped them into his mouth. He caught her staring as he was reaching to put it back. He paused.

"They're melatonin supplements," he said, pulling his hand back out of the cabinet, still holding the jar. "They don't work every time, but every now and again they'll let me fall back asleep." He smiled, a little embarrassed.

Jade nodded and gave him a small smile in return.

"Everything ok?" he asked as he put away the jar. "You're up pretty late too."

She nodded quickly and pointed timidly toward the half empty glass.

"I was just thirsty," she said, which was half the truth.

He nodded in acknowledgment but searched her face a moment longer, trying to see if there was anything she wasn't telling him about. But he wasn't going to push. It was too early in the morning for that.

"All right, well, I guess I should probably go and try to get some sleep," he said with a yawn. He started to make his way back toward his and Bennett's room. He paused at the entrance to the hallway and looked back to her. "You can stay up if you'd like; just turn this light off when you go back to bed."

Then he retreated down the hall, and Jade listened until she heard the soft click of his door closing.

VI

"I can do a little more than just move things around without actually touching them," Jade said to the two men who sat before her. The three of them sat around the small dinner table like they had the night before. Lewis had Bennett's hand gripped tightly in his own under the table. She stared down at her lap, not wanting to look at them when she spoke. It made it easier to talk about what she needed to talk about.

"I'm also able to heal myself," she started again, pausing, trying to find the words. "I don't know how it works, exactly, or if I can do it to other people too. I've never had to try." She started fidgeting with her fingers under the table, picking at the skin around her nails. "That's why I haven't been using the stick anymore."

Lewis and Bennett nodded along as she spoke. They had both noticed the absence of the makeshift crutch that morning (although Lewis was too sleep deprived the night before to make the connection when they had run into each other in the kitchen), but neither said anything. They both figured she'd say something about it eventually.

"So," Bennett ventured, "can I ask, how come you didn't just heal yourself right after you were hurt?" he asked slowly. "Why let it stay hurt for as long as you did?"

"Because I wasn't able to do it then," she answered quietly, still not looking up at them. "That ability was being blocked still. It takes a lot more out of me to heal myself than it does to move things around."

There was silence among them for a few minutes, and Jade knew they were—at least subconsciously—waiting for some kind of explanation. She took a deep breath and finally looked up.

"The people that were transporting me and the three others I was with injected us with serums that blocked our abilities," she explained. "They were designed to last the whole trip. But it didn't really end up working out that way." She muttered the last part. She could see shock forming in their eyes. Neither of the men knew what to think.

"Three others?" Lewis asked, a hint of something like concern in his voice. "There were others with you? *Like* you?"

"Yes. But I was the only one who escaped."

"What happened to them?"

Jade went quiet, looked down at her hands again. Tears began to fill her eyes as memories of that night—which felt like ages ago now—spun through her head. A rogue tear slipped down her cheek, and she rushed to get rid of it.

"They, uh—" she started, voice breaking. She cleared her throat and roughly wiped her face as another tear fell. "They didn't make it."

"Oh," Lewis breathed, squeezing his husband's hand even harder.

"We're sorry," Bennett said in a low voice. "For all that you've been through."

Jade smiled sadly and gave a weak laugh. She looked up at him, but only for a moment, before retreating her gaze.

"It's ok," she whispered.

"It isn't," Lewis said, wetness building in his own eyes. "But it will be."

Lewis was sitting on the porch swing, book open on his lap, when Bennett exited the cabin. He walked across the porch and leaned against the wooden railing. Lewis looked up from his book. He hadn't really been able to concentrate on anything he'd been reading and was constantly having to start a paragraph—or an entire page—over because his mind was elsewhere.

"Coffee?" Bennett asked, offering one of the two mugs he held in his hands.

Lewis smiled and took one. "Thanks."

They were quiet, and all that could be heard was the occasional singing of a faraway bird, or the rustling of leaves as a breeze swept the ground.

"What's Jade doing?" Lewis asked suddenly. Bennett sighed and put his free hand into the pocket of his jeans.

"Taking a nap," Bennett replied. "Kid's pretty beat."

Lewis nodded, taking a sip of his drink. The warmth of it crawled through his body quickly. "Don't blame her."

"Poor kid."

"I know," Lewis shook his head. "And she didn't even *begin* to really tell us about what these terrible people did to her. Or the other kids she was with." He closed his book and pulled his legs down off the swing to make room for Bennett, who gladly sat beside him.

Lewis laid his head on Bennett's shoulder and looped his left arm with Bennett's right. He turned the mug in his hands, thinking.

"What's up?"

"I'm worried."

"Worried? About what?"

Lewis's eyebrows pulled together. "I don't really know. All of it?" He answered. He knew it had something to do with Jade and the people who were after her. But that was a given. There was something else too. Something just felt...*off*. Like something was on its way to them. He didn't like it. Not at all.

VII

The trucks could be heard long before they could be seen. Their huge tires tore through fallen branches like they were nothing. When they reached the gravel driveway, it sounded like thunder was rumbling throughout the entire cabin. Lewis and Bennett stood from where they sat on the porch swing. Jade sat bolt upright in the guest room bed. All three of their hearts were pounding.

There were three of those giant trucks. One looked like it was covered in external armor. Its walls were two feet thick. Lewis's heart skipped a beat as the last vehicle came down the driveway and the two officers from the day before stepped out. They took a few steps toward the cabin, stopping about twenty feet away. The air buzzed all around them.

"Good afternoon, Mr. and Mr. Hayes." Officer White greeted them with a smile.

"Afternoon, officers. What's all this about?" Lewis asked, carefully snaking an arm around his husband. He felt like he was about to fall over. Bennett's thoughts were about Jade.

"Well, Mr. Hayes, we have a very good reason to believe that the missing girl we were asking about yesterday is somewhere here on the property," Officer O'Riley stated. His voice was much deeper than either of the men anticipated. It made him even more intimidating. Bennett's brows furrowed in fake confusion.

"Here? I think we'd have noticed if someone was here who shouldn't be. What makes you think she's here, of all places?" Officer White shrugged a little and shoved his hands in his pockets, putting all his weight to one side.

"We have our sources. Nothing to worry your little heads about."

A rage started to mix with the fear that was already in Lewis's belly. "Is all this necessary?" he asked calmly. "For one missing girl?"

White visibly sighed and glanced over at O'Riley.

"That's none of your concern now," Officer O'Riley replied flatly. "We need to conduct a search of the property."

As the words left his mouth, the back doors of the thick, armored truck swung open. Bennett started to sweat; Lewis's arm tightened around him.

Jade stood on the other side of the front door, listening and watching through the peephole. She saw the truck doors open. Her heart was beating out of her chest, and she was trying to think of something—anything—that could get them out of this.

One set of feet, then another, and then a few more spilled from the back of the truck. The gravel underfoot never sounded so ominous. A group of at least eight men in heavily armored gear rounded the back of the truck. A smaller figure stood guarded in the middle of the formation. The men on the porch could catch only glimpses of the white clothes behind the sea of black fabric. The formation stopped just behind the two officers.

"You have one chance, and one chance only to do this whole interaction peacefully," O'Riley called to them, crossing his arms over his chest. "You can give us the girl, or we will have no choice but to use force." Officer White made a gesture with his hand, and the formation of guards parted to reveal the figure they were hiding.

A child, much younger than Jade, and wearing the same clothes as the girl was found in, stood alone. His wrists were shackled with thick, electrified cuffs that were connected by a short chain to a collar made of the same material. His eyes were glued to the ground at his feet. His hair hung down over his face.

Oh god… Jade thought as she immediately recognized the small boy outside. *So that's how they found me.*

Outside, it was clear to the officers that the two men on the porch were going to make no move to hand over the girl. Why they were bothering to do this for a stranger, Officer White couldn't understand. But he was sure that if they knew what she was, they wouldn't be so keen. He turned his head slightly toward one of the guards at the front of the split formation.

"Go ahead," he said simply. Without hesitating, the armored man took three large steps toward the child and pushed a button on the collar around his neck. One by one, three green lights lit up before simultaneously turning red. The boy flinched as three separate syringes within the inner workings of the collar plunged into his throat and a murky red substance was administered.

It took a few moments before his entire demeanor changed. His shoulders squared, and his head slowly lifted to look at the cabin in front of him. As his head came up, his eyes rolled back. His body started to shake violently. His mouth hung open, but no sound came out. Two of the guards behind him held him upright as another came and unchained the cuffs around his wrists. Slowly he stilled. His eyes closed briefly, before shooting open to reveal eyes that were completely black, except for a small white dot where his pupils should be.

Lewis and Bennett stood petrified on the porch. Neither could move, and neither could look away from the scene unfolding before them. Officer White leaned as if he were going to say something to the little boy but stopped when a loud, metal creaking started to fill the air.

The trucks were raised a foot in the air before anyone noticed anything was happening. And they were slowly ascending. Eight, nine, ten feet; then they stopped. The air was still. Nothing and no one moved. No one even dared breathe as they stared—some in awe, others in horror—at the 100 tons of floating metal. It all happened in a blink.

The trucks slammed into one another. The sound and the impact of the explosion that followed sent everyone around it flying in different directions. As the heat from the fire was about to reach the cabin, Lewis and Bennett were grabbed by invisible hands and thrown backward through the front door that no one heard open. It slammed shut, and the cabin shook.

The two men stared blankly around them. None of it felt real. The sounds of agonized screams and raging fire outside told them otherwise. Lewis had Bennett's shirt held tightly in his hands, as if the slightest loosening of his grip would cause Bennett to disappear.

Jade's head swam. She was sitting on the floor by the front door, leaning against the wall. Her head was in her hands, her eyes closed tightly.

Bennett looked to Lewis. Neither of them had moved since being flung into the house. Lewis's eyes were glued to the front door, not really seeing it. It was more like he was looking through it, like he was still seeing what was going on outside.

"L," Bennett said softly, trying to get his husband's attention. The man beside him didn't move. "Lewis," he said, taking a hand and carefully turning Lewis's face until they were looking at each other. Lewis's eyes darted back and forth across Bennett's face.

"It's ok," Bennett said. "Deep breaths, Lewis, come on. We'll do them together, all right?" And they did. "In…and out, yep, that's it. Good job."

They did this until Lewis's fingers loosened their grip on Bennett's shirt just a little bit, and then finally let go. Bennett didn't know how he was able to stay so calm in this moment. But for Lewis, he'd shift the Earth.

"Jade," Bennett breathed, his thoughts suddenly returning to what this was all about in the first place. He spotted her where she sat and quickly crawled over to her. "Hey, kiddo," he said, placing a hand on her shoulder.

She was starting to get less dizzy, but she didn't open her eyes. She had never lifted that much weight all at once before. She hoped she wouldn't have to do it again any time soon.

"We need to get out of here," she said softly. "They know where I am now."

Bennett nodded, and he was trying to think of what to do. "Do you need me to do anything for you?" he asked.

She shook her head slowly. "No. I just need a minute."

"Ok." He paused. "Then I'm going to try to gather everything I think we'll need." With that, he stood and rushed toward the back of the cabin.

The little boy stood at the bottom of the porch steps, looking up blankly at the front door. Some of the lichen on the roof was smoldering; two of the front columns were ablaze. Behind him, bodies and pieces of the trucks were scattered all over the front yard. The local authorities who arrived later that night in response to a call about huge clouds of black smoke would find four bodies dangling from nearby trees, their flesh completely charred.

Officer O'Riley coughed as he dragged himself away from the burning rubble toward the far left side of the porch. His sunglasses were still on his face, but one of the lenses was gone. His face was covered in dirt and soot, and his left shoulder was dislocated. He scanned the entirety of the scene, and his eyes stopped on a familiar figure, lying flat on his back just thirty feet away.

"James?" Hurriedly O'Riley staggered to his feet, holding his injured arm. "James?" he repeated as he neared Officer White. He sank to his knees and stared blankly at his partner's body. The explosion had sent a baseball-sized chunk of metal through James White's chest, killing him instantly.

A rage started to build in the pit of O'Riley's stomach. He looked around him at the scene that had unfolded, and his anger grew. And grew. And grew. Until he saw the boy, standing dutifully at the bottom of the steps of the cabin, waiting for further instructions.

"Michael!" O'Riley screamed. The boy's head immediately whipped around to look at him and stopped, like an animatronic. "Get her!"

The cracking of bones sent a shiver down Officer O'Riley's spine. The young boy's body was contorting; bones were breaking and re-fusing, and skin was being stretched like elastic. A banshee-like shriek ripped through the air, and his small frame grew. And grew. Arms and legs doubled in length, tripled in strength. His torso elongated. The nails on his hands and feet formed into claws six inches long. His skin warped into a sickly gray color. All the hair on his body slowly released itself from his quickly changing form. O'Riley had never seen this transformation in person before. And he was horrified by the giant, monstrous, gray, skeletal figure that now stood in that small boy's place. The creature now stood—on all fours—breathing heavily. It sniffed the air.

The loud shriek on the other side of the front door made Jade's heart skip a beat. Her head shot up from her hands.

He's coming.

VIII

"What the hell was that?" Lewis asked from where he sat on the floor. He and Jade could both hear Bennett rummaging around in the back rooms of the cabin. He almost had three backpacks filled.

"We're running out of time. And that was our last warning." Jade groaned, slowly getting to her feet. She was much less dizzy now, but she didn't want to risk moving too fast—not until she had to. She offered Lewis her hand and helped him to his feet. Bennett suddenly came trotting down the hall toward them.

"Here," he said, offering a bag to each of them. "I grabbed what I could." A pair of pants, two shirts, a sweatshirt, and socks were rolled up and stuffed into the bottom of each backpack. From the guest room closet Bennett had grabbed two flashlights and put one in his own bag and the other in the bag he gave to Jade. A hunting knife and a map were placed in the front pocket of Lewis's bag. All the cash they kept in the house was in a plastic baggie that Bennett put into his own bag. It totaled about two thousand dollars.

There was a crash against the front door as they were securing their backpacks. The door frame shook.

"What is that?" Bennett asked, eyes darting back and forth between the door and the two people in front of him.

"There's no time to explain," Jade said, grabbing Bennett's right hand in her left, and Lewis's left hand in her right. "We need to go. *Now.*" And she dragged them toward the back door of the cabin.

Lewis had just stepped out of the back door—Jade close behind—when he suddenly turned around.

"Wait!" he whisper-shouted, not wanting to give their position away to whatever was trying to break in through the front door. "Benny, where's your gun?" Realization hit Bennett like a slap in the face.

"*Shit!*" Bennett groaned and retreated into the house. He ran as fast as he could back to his and Lewis's bedroom.

As he was reaching the doorway, another crash rattled the front door. The wood split and a bone-thin, gray arm reached through the hole in the door, its clawed hand thrashing and swiping at the air for anything it could get ahold of. The arm quickly snaked back through the hole, and the most horrifying face Bennett had ever seen slid into view. Its one visible eye darted here and there with a maddening quickness.

It's like looking up at the sky from the bottom of a hole, he thought immediately. It made Bennett's stomach turn in knots. The face moved back a little before sticking its nose through the broken wood and inhaling deeply.

Bennett had to force himself to keep moving. He ran to his side of the bed and grabbed the rifle where it stood propped against the wall. He then quickly rummaged through his bedside table for his spare box of bullets and sprinted out of the room. He could hear wood being torn apart behind him.

Lewis and Jade stood right outside of the back door, holding it open for him. The front door burst open—or at least what was left of the front door.

"Run!" Bennett shouted, and it was followed by the shrieking cry of the creature as it entered the house. The trio sprinted into the surrounding forest.

The creature tore through the house in pursuit of Jade. It blew through the kitchen, ransacked the living room, and finally found itself in the guest bedroom, where the scent was the strongest. With its claws, it destroyed the room looking for her.

The back door slammed shut with a sudden gust of wind, and the creature stopped. It left the room quickly, searching for the noise. As it went, Jade's scent got stronger again, and it plowed through the back door.

There was no sign of movement outside. The creature stood on all fours, scanning the area with its pit-like eyes. It suddenly stood up on its back legs, making its already very large frame that much bigger, and sniffed.

Bennett led the small group with a location in mind. Just a half-mile away from the cabin was a bomb shelter that the original owner had built during World War I. Why that crazy old guy had done it so far from his house, Bennett didn't know, but boy, was he glad for someplace to run to. Otherwise, he would have panicked, and they would all be dead by now. Killed by—well—whatever the hell that thing chasing them was.

"Where are we *going*?" Lewis huffed. Running had never been his strength, and he really hoped they weren't far from wherever Bennett was leading them. Jade ran alongside them, following blindly but trusting them.

Bennett didn't have time to answer. Behind them, much too close for comfort, they heard the shriek of the creature as it tore through the trees after them. *We're not gonna make it*, Bennett thought as he continued to run. He dared look behind them and saw nothing. Not yet. But it was gaining on them. *Quickly*.

Bennett knew they weren't going to make it in time. No way in hell. He stopped running, and the others stopped a few steps past him.

"What are you doing!" Lewis shouted, taking the few steps back to grab hold of Bennett's sleeve and start pulling him along. Bennett wouldn't budge. He quickly took his rifle off his shoulder. Jade stood, silently, watching.

"Honey," Bennett started, taking one of his hands and gently holding Lewis's face. "We're not gonna get there in time. That thing is already almost on us. But maybe if it's distracted, you two will have a chance," he said, looking from Lewis, to Jade, and then back to Lewis. The color drained from Lewis's face. His eyes darted behind Bennett, and then back to his face.

"Are you fucking insane?!" he screamed. He was terrified of what Bennett was proposing. Tears stung his eyes. Bennett only smiled, sadly.

"Probably," he answered with a slight shrug. "But that's also probably why you married me," he said. His own eyes were filling with tears. Lewis was shaking his head. The sounds of the pursuing creature were getting louder.

"We're not leaving you."

Bennett and Lewis both turned their heads to look at Jade. She stood about ten feet away from them. Dressed in a pair of Lewis's sweatpants and one of Bennett's T-shirts, she looked so small. So fragile. So *alone.*

"If anyone is sacrificing themselves, it's going to be me. I got you into this mess. I can't let you do this, Bennett," she paused, searching his face. "Not alone, at least."

Bennett gave her a small smile and nodded. "All right." He raised his rifle and cocked it.

The creature was on them now, and at any second it was going to come over a small hill, plowing through the underbrush. They could hear it tearing through the trees, knocking down some of the thinner ones.

Jade stood next to Bennett. Lewis stood just behind the two, the hunting knife now in his hand. They knew the thing was fast, but the speed at which it came over the hill still sent shivers down their spines. It was about 3,000 feet away. Bennett raised his gun.

Bennett could suddenly remember all the times he'd watched a movie and made fun of the guy who missed every shot he took at the monster that was running at him in a straight line. But he never had to feel the paralyzing terror, with his heart beating so hard he could hear it in his ears; *and it's deafening.* His hands shaking violently, and the pressure he can feel being put on him by the two figures beside him, even if they aren't meaning to put it there.

"I don't know how long I'll be able to hold it," Jade said from beside him. Her sudden voice almost made him jump out of his skin. "It might only be for a second."

He could barely hear her over the sound of his own heartbeat. He nodded.

2,000 feet.

"Are you ready?" Bennett heard himself ask. He saw her nod out of the corner of his eye. He raised the rifle and looked through the sight.

1,000 feet.

"On three." Jade took a deep breath. "One…two…three!"

The creature lunged. Time seemed to stop, only for a second, and he squeezed the trigger. The bullet plunged straight between the creature's pit-like eyes. Its body fell to the ground, tumbled, slid, and finally stopped two feet in front of them. There was a collective sigh, and Bennett was so relieved he could have passed out. Lewis was beside him in a second, wrapping an arm around Bennett's shoulders, holding on tightly.

The three watched in wonder as the creature's monstrous body quickly started to shift back into the form of the small boy from the truck. Lewis and Bennett turned their backs to the small, dead figure. Jade continued to stare. It felt unreal, seeing this little boy she'd met in the Lab, lying dead at her feet. Michael was four when he was brought to the Lab. Now she thought he, at eleven years old, was better off than she was. At least now he wouldn't have to live in fear. Wouldn't be weaponized. Hunted.

"Come on, Jade," Lewis called softly. "We've got to keep moving."

She turned and left Michael where he lay.

IX

It had taken them quite some time to get the door to the bomb shelter open. Bennett had to use the butt end of this rifle to break the padlock free, and it took a good deal of pulling to get the rusty hinges to move. With the flashlight from his backpack, Bennett led them down ten steps (he couldn't help but count them). There was a pull string hanging just a foot ahead of him, and he held his breath as he lightly tugged.

A soft yellow light illuminated the small room. The shelter was about the size of an average college dorm room. A bunk bed sat against the far wall to the left of the stairs, and a small twin bed sat along the adjacent wall. To the right was a floor-to-ceiling shelf that was stocked full of canned goods, jugs of water, blankets, clothes, cookware, and various other items. The trio was amazed. Lewis let out a whistle and Bennett nodded his head in agreement.

"This has been here the whole time?" Lewis asked.

"Yeah, I guess so. I remember the Realtor telling us about it when we bought the cabin, but I honestly forgot about it until today. Never thought we'd come all the way out here."

Bennett turned to face Jade where she stood, just behind the couple.

"Which one would you like?" he asked, gesturing to the three bed options.

"I guess I'll take this one," she pointed to the lone twin bed. Bennett turned to Lewis and grinned.

"Looks like we get the bunk bed," he said, wiggling his eyebrows.

"I call top bunk!" Lewis shouted and slipped past Bennett. He threw his backpack up on the bed, quickly climbed the ladder, and flopped down onto the rickety mattress. Bennett stood there with his mouth hanging open.

"You didn't even give me a chance!" he mock-complained, shuffling over to the bottom bunk and setting his backpack on the floor. Lewis peeked over the thin railing and gave a little shrug.

"You snooze you lose, Benny. That's just the way things go." Bennett gasped and it turned into a laugh. Lewis failed to contain the grin that grew on his face.

Outside, the sky was dark, and the only sounds were crickets chirping and an owl that hooted in the distance. Inside, they ate warmed up chicken soup from paper bowls. Jade sat cross-legged on her bed; Lewis and Bennett sat shoulder to shoulder on the bottom bunk. Both men had noticed that Jade had been quiet since the whole situation with that monster—with that little boy.

Of course, Jade hadn't spoken a whole lot since they first met her. But this seemed a little different. Like she was thinking. Or trying *not* to think. But the two of them were so *curious.* They wanted—*needed*—to know more about everything that was going on. About her. And so, Lewis finally asked.

"Did you know him?"

He felt stupid for asking it, because it was obvious by her silence, and the way she had stood there after he was killed, that she'd known him. But he didn't know how else to start. She remained silent for a moment. She pushed the soup around with her spoon.

"Yeah," she finally said. "I knew him." She placed the bowl down on the bed beside her. "His name was Michael. He was one of the kids from the Lab."

Lewis and Bennett also put their bowls to the side, the latter placing a hand on his husband's knee. They buzzed with anticipation, and they were scared—and embarrassingly excited—to learn more. This had simultaneously been the most dangerous and most exciting days of their lives. And they knew it wasn't going to stop any time soon. They hoped Jade couldn't tell all of that from how they looked, sitting across from her.

"Were you always with these people who are after you?" Bennett asked. "This 'Lab'?" She shook her head.

"No. I was an orphan living in a run-down home when they took me. I think that's how they get all of us." She paused. "They go around to orphanages that are closing, or in desperate need of money, and they take a kid or two who would otherwise be sent to some other home." Her brows furrowed and she glared down at her lap where her hands sat, fingers picking at the skin around her nails. "I was ten when they took me." The couple sat quietly, letting that information soak into their brains.

"And have you always been able to—well, I mean—do the things you do?" Bennett asked. She looked up at them.

"No," she said almost in a whisper, fingers still picking. "None of us could." It was the answer that they dreaded to hear but knew was coming.

"I see."

"So, they…what? *Experimented* on children?" Lewis asked incredulously. She nodded.

"Yes," she answered. "That's exactly what they did. It's much easier for them to take people no one wanted or would go looking for, in order to do what they do." An ache settled in all their hearts. It seemed that everyone felt unwanted at some point or another. Tears started to build in Jade's eyes, and she quickly wiped them away.

"You don't have to tell us any more if you don't want to."

"But I *do* want to," she sighed, a tear slipping down her cheek. "It's just—" her voice cracked. "It hurts to remember."

Lewis swallowed hard. Bennett's heart was hammering in his chest, and his hands shook just a little bit.

"We understand," he said, thankful that his voice was steadier than his hands. "It's ok." Jade nodded, tried to sit up straighter, and took a few deep breaths. She *wanted* to tell them. *Somebody* had to know what was going on at the Lab.

"They'd take us blindfolded from our rooms to even bigger rooms with white walls. And there was one wall that reflected the whole room, making it look even bigger. Scarier. They'd strap you into this big metal chair and inject you with the serums," she started again, talking kind of fast. She figured if she spoke a little faster, she'd be able to keep herself from crying. "Every week it was something new. A new formula that the team created. And they would try them out, every single one, until something finally clicked." The fast talking was working so far. "As far as I know, not every serum is able to work for every test subject. So the serum that worked on me wouldn't have worked on Michael. They always said it had something to do with our brain chemistry, or something like that. They never really talked directly to any of us. Most of what I know is just stuff I've overheard them discussing with each other.

"And once they found the one that worked for you, that's all they would give you. They wanted to see the full extent of whatever it was that that serum unlocked. I don't think they ever had any idea what any of the serums were supposed to do. Sometimes I wonder if some weren't really serums at all. That they just wanted to stab us with needles and watch us squirm." She stopped a moment, thinking. "I'm pretty sure that of all of us they gave a second serum to, I'm the only one it had any effect on."

Lewis hesitated then asked, "Is that why they were taking you away from the Lab? When you escaped?" She thought quietly for a second, and then slowly shook her head.

"I don't think so. There were three others with me who were also being taken somewhere else. None of them had had a second. I have no idea why we were being moved. Or where we were going."

X

Thirty miles away from the bomb shelter, in a small, vacant motel, Thomas O'Riley sat on a bed drinking whiskey straight from the bottle. His left arm was held useless by a sling. The little box TV sat untouched; its black screen reflected the entirety of the motel room: the faded yellow and brown striped walls, the weird blue carpet, and the one queen bed. A tall lamp that was missing its shade stood in the corner by the window. A small bedside table sat to the right of O'Riley. On top of that was a phone. It rang.

He groaned as he put the bottle down harshly and picked up the receiver.

"Hello?"

"Is this Thomas O'Riley?"

"Yup."

"Good, I'm glad I got the right number. This is Doctor Julian Peters." O'Riley sat up straighter in the bed, his fingers tightening on the handle of the phone.

Shit.

Julian Peters is the head scientist at the Lab. The one responsible for the experimentation and transport of the children. O'Riley scowled. *If you could even call them children at this point*. He cleared his throat.

"Yes, sir. How are you, sir?"

"I've had better days; I won't lie to you. And I know you have as well. I'm sorry for your loss, Officer O'Riley." Thomas's throat tightened, and a pang of sadness and anger—and was that guilt?—formed in his chest. He squeezed his eyes shut and cleared his throat once more.

"Thank you, sir." There was a pause on the other end of the line.

"Well, I guess I'll get straight to the point then," Doctor Peters began. "I'm calling regarding the failure to transport and complete the capture of Jade Cooper." Thomas's heart was pounding in his chest. His head throbbed. "I see in the report here that there was quite an extensive team, including the use of the child Michael Weston, most of whom were either killed or terribly injured. And there is no report of Michael ever returning to the Lab. Do you know why that is?"

Thomas opened his eyes and glanced around the room absently.

"No, sir," he finally answered. And he really didn't. The last time he saw Michael was when his strange, monstrous form entered the cabin. But the collar around his throat had a built-in tracker. It would only cease to work if the wearer took it off or died while wearing it.

"I was afraid of that," Doctor Peters said almost too quietly for Thomas to hear. There was a sigh on the other end of the line. "I'm putting in the command for Protocol 42."

Thomas's eyes widened in surprise, and he stood from the bed. His head swam for a second, and he wished he'd gotten this phone call before he'd started drinking.

"But what about the other protocols?" Thomas questioned. He wasn't expecting the doctor to jump so far ahead.

"The situation is already too out of hand," Doctor Peters began. "It should have been treated as a level six disaster the moment she was able to set foot off that truck. I'm going to call first thing tomorrow morning and have the order set."

There was silence on both lines. Peters was waiting for some kind of response, and O'Riley was trying to soak up all this information into his brain, which was getting drunker and drunker by the minute.

"What do you need me to do?" he finally asked. Doctor Peters made a sound that made Thomas think he was shrugging.

"Well, first I suppose I needed to know if you were even interested in staying a part of this endeavor. What with your injury and the loss of your partner."

"I'm in," Thomas blurted out. "Whatever you need me to do, I'm there."

Doctor Peters grinned on the other end of the phone. "Perfect. Then here's what I need you to do."

XI

The map was spread out across the single twin bed, its edges held down by two cans of peaches, a flashlight, and a stack of used paper bowls. Bennett looked over it, trying to locate exactly where the bomb shelter was. He chewed on the eraser of a pencil he'd found in the bunker. He already had the cabin circled on the map.

Bennett was trying to come up with a plan of action. They couldn't just stay here forever. He made a rough calculation, and circled where he thought they were on the folded paper. Lewis walked over with a paper cup steaming with black coffee.

"What are you thinking?" he asked, kneeling on the floor beside Bennett. He offered the cup, but Bennett shook his head.

"I'm trying to think of where we can go from here. There's not really anything close."

Lewis nodded, sipped his drink. "What about your mom's old place?" he suggested. With his free hand, he pointed to a spot on the map about twenty miles north of where Bennett had drawn the circles.

"That's kind of far though, don't you think? To walk all that way?" Bennett asked. He paused to chew on the eraser, mulling the idea over. "And besides, who's to say someone hasn't bought the place yet?"

"That's fair," Lewis agreed. "But distance is going to be our best friend for a while. I think it'd be worth a shot. Plus, there are a lot of other places around her old house. If it doesn't work there, we wouldn't have to go very far to find someplace else."

Bennett thought for a while. He hadn't been to that house in almost a decade. The property has been vacant (as far as he knew) since she passed. He didn't even think that any of her stuff was ever taken out. It might all still be there. Stuck in time.

"I mean, is there anything else you can think of?" Lewis asked, pulling Bennett back to the present. Bennett sighed and shook his head. Lewis wrapped an arm around his husband's shoulders and gave him a squeeze. "It'll work out, love. We'll figure something out."

Bennett nodded and leaned his head against Lewis's shoulder.

Eight hundred miles from the bomb shelter, Thomas O'Riley sat, waiting to be called into the director's office. His head throbbed, and his shoulder didn't feel any better. His flight has been delayed twice in the process of getting here, and he'd barely gotten enough sleep to deal with *anything* today, let alone any kind of meeting.

The hall was busy with people, their passing voices much too loud for his liking. He'd already been waiting over an hour, and he was starting to grow impatient.

Doctor Peters had called him in his hotel room early this morning—after putting in the call for Protocol 42—

to tell him that he was to meet with the man who was put in charge of the operation: Director Joshua Harris. What they were going to talk about, O'Riley didn't know. It was too sensitive to be briefed over the phone.

The office door opened, and out stepped a young woman in a black knee-length skirt, and white blouse. She had a clipboard carrying a thick file resting on her hip.

"Mr. O'Riley?" she called, scanning the hall. It was only now that Thomas even noticed that four other men had joined him in his waiting. He stood and the young woman gave him a welcoming smile.

"Good afternoon, sir. Director Harris is ready to see you now."

Thomas said nothing, just nodded stiffly. She held the door open for him, and they walked into what looked like a very small office. There was a short desk, one chair behind the desk and two in front, three filing cabinets, and an oval rug on the floor. A closed laptop sat in the middle of the desk, and two stacks of papers were piled neatly on the front edges. At the far end of the small room was a wooden door with a silver plaque that read: Director Joshua Harris.

Why I couldn't have just waited in here instead of in that loud ass hallway, I'll never understand, he thought as the young woman led him across the room and softly knocked on the second office door.

"Come in," a muffled voice called from the other side. The young woman opened the door and let Thomas inside.

Behind a much bigger desk than the one in the other room sat the director. His desk was littered with papers, knick-knacks, and small framed photos. A large computer screen took up most of the space on the right side of the desk. The director stood to greet them, rounding the desk and reaching out his hand to Thomas.

"Mr. O'Riley, I presume?" he asked, and Thomas took his hand to shake.

"Yes, sir."

Director Harris glanced over at the young woman, who proceeded to hand him the large file attached to her clipboard.

"Thank you, Jackie, that'll be all."

She smiled and left the office, closing the door securely behind her.

"Take a seat," Director Harris said, gesturing to two chairs as he went around and sat in his own, opening a drawer and dropping the file inside. Thomas sat, using his good arm to ease himself into the chair.

"So, Doctor Peters has informed me of the events leading up to the demand for Protocol 42," he began. He leaned on his elbows, folding his hands over scattered pages. "As you know, I have been placed in charge of this operation. What I need from you today is as much information as you can give me." He leaned back in his chair. "I want you to tell me about the failed transportation from the beginning to the end."

Thomas's head spun momentarily. He wasn't expecting this meeting to start so quickly. But he wasn't too surprised, considering what was at stake.

"Sure," he said, clearing his throat and adjusting in his seat. "The transportation was set to begin on November 13, and we were scheduled to reach our destination on November 15 of this year. The four subjects were first sedated and then injected with the Blocker serum in their quarters. Once they were all unconscious, they were cuffed hand and foot and wheeled out to the trucks via gurneys.

"The sedation was supposed to last through the first day, which it did, successfully. But the Blockers were supposedly designed to last the entire three-day trip. During the second night, on November 14, at 0100 hours, the guards from truck 309 alerted the rest of the band of suspicious activity between the two subjects being transported in that vehicle. The man who reported the issue, Lucas Donovan, said that he'd heard the two conspiring.

"The trucks were stopped at 0105 hours, and the subjects were evacuated from the vehicles. They were positioned in a line, shoulder to shoulder.

"All four subjects were questioned by Dane Richards, the head of the operation. Officer James White and I stood nearby, watching the interaction. Neither of us was there to interact with the subjects at all. We were simply assigned to deal with civilians or law enforcement if ever a problem arose during the transport.

"All of them denied the accusations of planning an escape. The subjects from 308 were believed to be telling the truth. But there was no denying that the ones from 309 were lying. These two were the pyrokinetic, Justin Matthews, and the Mind Manipulator, Emily Reed.

Zachary Reynolds, the necrokinetic, and Jade Cooper, the telekinetic, were being escorted back to 308 when the altercation took place."

"Hold on a second," Director Harris interrupted leaning on his desk. "I'm sorry, but I don't really know what some of these 'kinetic' words mean. I'm afraid I'm not too educated in the scientific language of the Lab."

"Yes, of course," O'Riley said, trying to contain a smirk. It made him feel powerful, in a way, knowing things that this man—who was now his new boss—didn't. "Allow me to explain. Pyrokinesis is the manipulation of fire by will of the mind. Justin Matthews could conjure fire and flames simply by thinking about it.

"Necrokinesis is the manipulation of the dead. Zachary Reynolds could quite literally wake the dead. Now, of course, they were not restored to their healthy, living selves. They were merely walking corpses—very much like zombies, if you will. But Zachary could control them as well as wake them from eternal sleep.

"And finally, telekinesis. Telekinesis is the ability to move and manipulate objects by will of the mind. As far as the Lab knows, there is no limit to how much a telekinetic can move or manipulate all at once."

Director Harris nodded with O'Riley's explanations. "Understood," he said, and gave a slight wave of his hand. "Please, continue." O'Riley nodded and adjusted in his seat once more.

"The altercation happened quickly. One moment, the subjects Reynolds and Cooper were being taken back to the truck, with Matthews and Reed remaining for further interrogation, and the next, a gunshot rang through the woods and everyone went into a panic. It was as if I'd blinked my eyes and the entire world flipped upside down.

"Dane Richards said later that he'd fired the gun because he saw—or *thought* he saw—Matthews reaching for the gun of the man standing guard right next to him. I'm sure Justin Matthews hit the ground before he even knew what had happened to him. He was dead instantly; shot through the heart.

"After that, everyone else who'd been positioned close to the subjects started firing their guns. Officer White and I immediately took to the ground, trying to get out of the line of fire, and to see what exactly was going on.

"I watched Emily Reed quickly take hold of the arms of two guarding men beside her and whisper something to each of them. I was shocked to see one raise his gun and start shooting at the other men. The other one took a key from his belt and undid the locks on both pairs of her cuffs.

"I knew then that the Blocker serums weren't working as effectively as the scientists from the Lab said they would and that this subject had just used her mind controlling abilities. The first man under her influence had killed three men before his comrades took notice and shot him down.

"I watched Reed take the key from the second man—who was gunned down moments later by a stray bullet—

and run to where the other two subjects stood, cowering against the chaos taking place in front of them.

"In an instant I was on my feet with my gun in my hands. I could feel Officer White beside me, trying to pull me back down and out of the line of bullets. Ignoring him, I aimed and fired. The first bullet caught Reed just below the ribs, and she staggered forward but didn't lose her footing. I fired again as she was about to reach the other two, this time hitting her right lung. She fell forward, the key flying from her hands toward the other subjects, who were now standing only three or so feet from where she fell.

"The smaller boy, Zachary Reynolds, immediately jumped forward for the key. I raised my gun again and fired, hitting him in the throat.

"Now Jade Cooper stood alone, looking horrified at the scene going on around us. The other guards were still shooting at each other, unaware that the original enemy had already been eliminated. No one paid any attention to her. No one but me.

"Then she looked up, finally seeing me. She made the slightest movement, and the gun in my hand crumpled, like a tin can being crushed between my fingertips. I dropped it, horrified, and watched it fall, disfigured, to the grass at my feet. It had only been five seconds that I stared down at that gun, but by the time I looked up again, she was gone. Disappeared. Like she'd never been there in the first place.

"Eight men and three of the four subjects were killed that night. When the chaos had finally calmed, the men who were left were immediately sent into the woods to search for her, but with no success." Thomas stopped, watching the Director who had been nodding—probably subconsciously—throughout the whole retelling. His brows were pulled together in the middle of his forehead, giving him a puzzled, or maybe a bit more of a concerned, expression. They sat silently for a very long three minutes.

"Do you need me to recount the events that took place at the cabin once we located her, sir?" Thomas finally asked, breaking the silence that was beginning to irritate him. Director Harris shook his head, and that concerned, puzzled look disappeared from his face.

"No, Mr. O'Riley, that'll do."

"Yes, sir."

"Well," the director began, releasing a heavy sigh, "I do suppose that is all I will be requiring of you today." He rose from his chair. O'Riley did the same. The director led him to the second office door, and they walked through Jackie's office, where the young woman sat at her small desk, typing on her laptop. As they entered, she stood and walked to the main door, opening it to let them out.

The loudness of the hall buzzed around O'Riley's head like an annoying swarm of bees. Director Harris extended his hand for a shake, which O'Riley took dutifully.

"I have some arranging to do in preparation for Protocol 42, but I will give you a call when we're ready to move forward."

Thomas nodded and gave him a friendly smile. "Thank you, sir. I look forward to working with you, sir."

Director Harris retreated into the joint offices, and the young woman politely bid him a good afternoon before retreating herself. O'Riley held the smile until the door had securely closed, and then he immediately dropped it. He turned and made his way to the exit and out onto the street, where he'd hail a cab back to his hotel, where he'd wait for further instruction.

XII

"Protocol 42: designed to handle high intensity, extremely classified, global emergencies. Information leaks regarding the process, setup, or reasoning for such action is punishable by execution.

"This means that if any one of you talks about this operation with anyone who is not involved, you will be killed, and they will along with you. We do not care if it is your closest friend, your spouse, your children, or anyone else that you may tell your deepest, darkest secrets to. If you care about them and their lives at all, you will not speak, or even dare *think*, about this operation in their presence. Is that understood?"

There was unanimous agreement throughout the small auditorium. Director Harris looked out over the one hundred and fifty people who had been assigned. Some he recognized from previous years. Others were as green to this kind of work as you can be. He could see it in the way they squirmed in their chairs when he made it clear just how intense the operation was. Director Harris fed on it.

"Very well," he said, straightening his posture and pressing the button that turned on the overhead projector. "Let's begin."

Nine hours after the trio had left the bunker, they finally came to the paved driveway that led to Bennett's late mother's home. Before leaving the bomb shelter, they had filled their packs with as much food and other necessities as they could. Lewis and Bennett also carried jugs of water. They had stopped four times, about a half hour each time, to refuel themselves, go to the bathroom, or simply give their aching legs a break.

Anxiety, heavy like a stone, made a home in Bennett's chest as they went down the long driveway. It was surrounded by trees on both sides, making it impossible to see the house from the road. He was still worrying that they'd finally gotten here after walking all this time and were about to find people living inside, and they'd have to keep going. But as they got closer to the house, he saw that there were no cars or any other signs of other people. He was hopeful. Then they rounded the last turn and he saw that the for-sale sign was still posted in the yard. Moss covered most of it, making it harder to read.

The house itself was almost completely overtaken by climbing vines; the little bit of grass that grew around the house reached to the middle of their calves. White paint flaked off weathered walls, and moss and lichen had completely claimed the roof—not a shingle in sight.

Dead leaves were scattered across the porch. It was almost haunting how abandoned it was.

"Here we are," he announced to the other two, who were following a couple of feet behind.

Lewis groaned. "There's no way I'm going to be able to walk tomorrow," he muttered.

Bennett rolled his eyes and chuckled lightly. "Just a minute or two longer, and we'll be able to get inside. I just need to find a key." He set his backpack and the jugs of water down in the dirt at his feet and stretched his arms up above his head. His spine made sickening—but much appreciated—pops. He sighed, relieved to be rid of the weight for at least a few minutes.

Lewis set his things down as well; Jade continued to hold hers. They watched Bennett walk around to the back of the house. They could hear his feet shuffling through the leaves even after he disappeared.

Bennett hoped that the fake rock would still be where it had been for the past twenty-five years. He remembered the day his mother bought it and how she'd thought it to be "the darndest thing." She had liked clever things like that.

He missed her.

He had to move a great deal of dead leaves around before he finally found it. The originally gray-painted rock was now almost black with dirt and had green stuff growing all over it. If it hadn't still felt like plastic, he would have easily mistaken it for a real rock. He picked it up with ease and turned it over to reveal the secret compartment. He removed the key, a little rusty, and set it back in its place.

He grinned at Lewis and Jade as he came back to the front of the house where they waited. He wasn't at all surprised to see Lewis was sitting on top of his backpack, seemingly unable to remain standing for a single second longer than he needed to.

"Come on, L, get up." Bennett chuckled, lightly grabbing hold of Lewis's arm and pulling him up. Lewis was not afraid to protest in the slightest. He moaned and groaned, saying he could no longer feel his legs and that Bennett was going to have to carry him inside or he'd end up getting eaten by a bear because he wouldn't be able to run away. Jade covered a smile with her hand, muffling her giggles. Bennett rolled his eyes and let go of his husband's arm to grab his own backpack and jugs of water and made his way up the stairs and onto the porch. Jade followed, and after a few moments Lewis got up and climbed the stairs too.

"I can't believe you were just going to let me die out here," he mumbled as Bennett put the key in the lock. Bennett held his breath as he turned it and sighed, relieved, when the old lock clicked. He opened the door, and they entered the house.

A thick layer of dust covered just about everything. As they walked across the floor, their shoes left behind footprints. *Like walking in the snow*, Lewis thought. He suddenly wondered if Jade had ever gotten a chance to experience a real snow day before she'd been taken. For a moment, a pang of sadness made a home in his chest.

He felt *bad* for her. *Really* bad. She's had a lot taken from her and never knew what she was missing.

Jade's eyes searched the inside of the home restlessly, looking for anything that might scream: *Danger! Leave now!* She wanted to enjoy this place, to take in the large living room and the stairs that led up to a loft in all its beautiful artistry, the walls covered in shelves, fully stacked with books and picture frames, the fireplace with its stone border, the large couch and two love seats that, even with all the dust, looked like the most comfortable places on Earth. But *they* had found her once. It was only a matter of time before *they* found her again. She couldn't help but turn that knowledge over in her mind until it was smooth, any doubt or hope that it might not happen worn away. Because it will. It always does.

She walked over to one of the shelves as Lewis and Bennett were setting their things down in the open kitchen just under the loft. She picked up the first picture her eyes fell upon.

It was of a young boy—*Looks like Michael's age*—and an older woman. They were smiling, and she could see what appeared to be a very large body of water behind them. The boy's cheeks were bright pink, and one of his bottom teeth was missing. Jade set the frame back into place and looked at the next one. The same boy from before—maybe a little older now—stood in a patch of red dirt with a helmet on his head and a bat hanging from his right hand. He was smiling, but it didn't quite reach his eyes like the last one did. She moved on to the next picture.

In this one, the boy was much older, wearing a long blue robe and matching cap, holding a piece of paper in one hand, his other arm wrapped around the shoulders of the same woman from the first photo—who also looked much older.

The last picture on the shelf had two figures that Jade could recognize. It was a picture of Lewis and Bennett wearing matching black tuxes and matching black bowties. They were holding each other in their arms, both smiling big smiles. She turned toward the kitchen, where the couple were unpacking their backpacks.

"Are these pictures of you?" she asked, causing them both to look up from what they were doing.

Lewis grinned and looked over at an already blushing Bennett. He felt embarrassed having his picture taken. He felt even more embarrassed when people *saw* the pictures of him.

Bennett scratched at the beard on his face. "Yeah," he said, walking around the kitchen counter and into the living room where she stood. "They sure are." He picked up the picture of him and the woman at the beach. "This is my mom," he said, turning the frame to show her. "I think I was, what—ten years old here?" He went silent for a moment, staring at the picture, thinking. He set it down and picked up the next one. The one of him in the baseball uniform. The one in which his smile didn't reach his eyes.

"I hated playing baseball," he said with a light laugh. "But my mom wanted me to play a sport, so I figured 'Hey, I like to watch baseball, maybe I'll enjoy playing it too.'" He stopped, shaking his head and still laughing a little. He put the photo down and turned to her. "Too much running, if you ask me. You don't get as tired from just watching."

Jade smiled a little. She glanced back at the pictures. "Are there more?"

"Pictures?"

She nodded.

"Well, I'm sure my mom had a whole collection of them around here somewhere," he answered, rubbing the back of his neck as he subconsciously looked around the room, as if a box of photographs and albums would suddenly appear there in the living room. "I guess I could try to find them."

"Would you?"

His arm fell to his side again, and he couldn't help but grin at her. She'd totally lit up at the idea of seeing more pictures. How could he refuse?

"Sure thing, kid. I'll search for them in a little bit."

They walked together to the kitchen, where Lewis was putting things away in cupboards.

"I wish I had pictures."

XIII

Lewis found Bennett in his mother's old room, sitting on the bed. He'd said he was going to look for the photos fifteen minutes ago, after he'd come back inside. He'd gone out to the back shed to turn on the generator his mom had had to see if it still had any juice after all this time. Thankfully, it did.

Lewis saw that Bennett had opened the blinds in the room and was sitting facing the window with his back to the door. Outside, the sky was painted with shades of pink, orange, and blue. Bennett's shoulders shook slightly, and a tightness formed in Lewis's chest. He gave a very soft knock to the door. Bennett turned and wiped away the wetness in his eyes.

"Hey," Bennett said with a sniff, shifting how he sat so that he was facing Lewis where he stood.

Lewis gave him a sad smile. "Hey." He walked over to the bed and sat down next to Bennett. He sat quietly for a moment, watching him. "You ok?" He asked. But he knew the answer. Bennett sighed and looked down at his hands.

"I just never thought I'd come back here again." Bennett said quietly. "And it's all here, just as she left it." A tear slipped down his face. Lewis sighed and wrapped an arm around him. Bennett laid his head on Lewis's shoulder. "I really miss her."

"I know, Benny," Lewis said, squeezing Bennett tighter. "I know." Bennett's body started to tremble as sobs overtook him.

"I should have been here," he choked. "I should have come to say goodbye."

Lewis closed his eyes, resting his chin on top of Bennett's head. He knew the guilt Bennett held over himself for not going to see his mother when she was dying. He hated that Bennett couldn't forgive himself. His mother surely had.

Bennett's sobs finally ceased after a few minutes. They sat there for a while, on the edge of the bed, Lewis holding him, staring out the window at the sun going down. Bennett sighed but didn't move.

"Thanks," he whispered. Lewis hummed and lightly kissed the top of Bennett's head.

"Of course, love."

Bennett finally sat up, glancing at the bedroom door. "I guess we'd better find those pictures and get back out there, huh?" Lewis smiled at him softly.

"If that's what you wanna do."

Bennett nodded.

"All right then," Lewis said, standing and holding his hand out for Bennett to take, which he did. "Let's go on a picture hunt."

The three of them sat on the big couch in the living room, Bennett in the middle with Jade and Lewis on either side of him. The shades and curtains over all the windows were drawn tightly. Lewis had gotten the fire going in the fireplace. There were lamps on either side of the couch that were turned on so they could see the albums clearly. Lewis and Bennett had found the books hidden in the crawlspace under the stairs.

They flipped through the pages slowly, with Bennett describing what was going on in most of them. He smiled and pointed at a picture of him and four other boys. They stood with their backs to a large swimming pool. They were all soaked, their hair plastered to their foreheads. Arms were draped over shoulders.

"These were friends of mine from middle school," he explained. "My friend Adam here," he pointed to the boy in the middle of the group, "had a pool party for his thirteenth birthday. There were *at least* ten kids there. But the five of us were best buddies."

"Do you still talk to any of them?" Jade asked.

"No, most of us kind of grew apart after high school. I still hung out with Adam for a couple of years after we started college, but then life took over and we grew apart too. It was unfortunate, really." His face fell for a moment but quickly went back to normal. Lewis placed a hand on Bennett's shoulder and rested his head there. A few more pages were flipped.

"What about this one?" Jade pointed. It was a much older photo. In it, a man held a little bundle in his arms, the face of a baby just visible in the sea of white fabric. The man smiled brightly at the child in his arms.

"That's my dad," Bennett said, a sad smile on his face. "This was taken the day I was born."

Jade looked away from the photo and at Bennett. "That baby is *you*?"

Bennett laughed and nodded his head. He flipped a few more pages, telling little stories about school field trips, vacations he went on with his mother, more birthday parties.

Jade's brows furrowed and she looked at Bennett again. She felt a bit of anxiety asking her next question. "How come your dad isn't in any of these pictures?" she asked, just above a whisper.

Bennett went quiet for a second. "He passed away shortly after I was born." He finally said. "He was killed in a car accident when I was three months old." Lewis gave Bennett's shoulder a light squeeze. Jade looked back down at the album.

"Sorry," she said, starting to pick at her hands. "I shouldn't have asked that."

Bennett quickly looked at her. "No, it's fine." He assured her. "It's ok to ask." She nodded but didn't look up at him.

There were three rooms in the house, including the loft. Lewis and Bennett let Jade pick where she'd like to sleep. Unknown to her, she had ended up picking Bennett's mother's room. Which, of course, Bennett was completely fine with. He wasn't really surprised. That room seemed to have some kind of magnetic pull to it.

And he didn't think that he really wanted to sleep in there anyway.

The couple now sat on a cushioned bench out on the back patio. Jade had retired to bed two hours ago. It was cold outside, but not bitter cold. There was no wind to bite at any exposed skin. They each held a cup of coffee, partially to drink and partially to keep their hands warm. There was plenty of room on the bench for them to each have a cushion to sit on, but they still sat shoulder to shoulder. Behind the house were mostly trees, but there was also a decent sized stream that flowed across from left to right. Silently they sat, listening to the water gurgle over stones.

"You doin' ok?" Lewis asked suddenly.

Bennett nodded and smiled over at Lewis. "Yeah, I'm all right."

"Good." Lewis entangled one of his arms with one of Bennett's. He thought for a moment before speaking again.

"How long do you think we have?" he asked. Like Jade, they both knew it was only a matter of time before people came looking and found her again. Bennett sighed, shaking his head slowly.

"I guess there's no way to tell," he began. "For all we know they could have already figured out where we were going. They could be coming up the driveway *right now.*" He knew it wasn't true, and Lewis did too. But it still scared them.

When they first heard the commotion inside, they just assumed Jade had gotten up and was getting some water. But a loud banging sent them jumping up off the bench and sprinting inside. Both of them immediately thought that they'd all been found, that people were in the house after Jade. But as they entered the house, they noticed that nothing in the living room indicated that anyone had broken in. There was silence, and they stood listening, waiting for another noise. Bennett looked over to Lewis, a puzzled expression on his face. They were both out of breath.

"What the hell—"

Another bang, loud enough to shake the walls, came from down the hall, where the bedrooms were. They hesitated, only for a moment, before running down the hall and throwing Jade's door open.

Hovering three feet off the ground was every piece of furniture in the room; except for the bed where Jade slept. She was twisting and turning and muttering incoherent sentences, but she was clearly asleep. The dresser near the door suddenly dropped, slamming into the hardwood and throwing the few things that were still on top of it onto the floor. A few seconds passed before it started to rise again.

The couple stood in the doorway, dumbfounded. They both jumped as a lamp in the far corner of the room suddenly dropped, landing flat on the floor. The bulb popped and glass scattered across the floor. The lamp did not rise in the air again. Jade continued to move restlessly.

"Jade?" Lewis called, trying (but not very hard) to wake her. He knew they would probably have to go over to the bed to wake her up. But he also didn't want either of them to get crushed by furniture. Bennett went to take a step inside the room and Lewis grabbed his arm.

"Wait a second," he said, before disappearing a little farther down the hall into their room and returning seconds later holding both pairs of their shoes. "You don't want to step in the glass." Bennett nodded and they both donned their shoes before carefully entering.

The air in the room felt like it was vibrating. It made the hairs all over their bodies stand on end as they approached the bed. Jade's face was slick with sweat; her hairline was soaked. She had completely kicked the comforter off the bed with her constant thrashing. She continued to mutter as Bennett slowly sat on the edge of the bed. He hesitated. The bedside table next to him suddenly dropped to the floor, and he almost jumped out of his skin. His heart was pounding in his chest. He reached his hand out and gently shook Jade's shoulder.

"Jade," he called, trying to be gentle, but also needing her to wake up. "Jade, wake up." He shook her shoulder again, a little harder, and her eyes flew open. That single action scared Bennett almost as much as it scared Jade to see him sitting there in front of her. She inhaled sharply and scrambled to sit up in the bed. Everything that was still levitating immediately fell to the floor in one huge bang, which frightened her even more. Her eyes darted around the darkened room, searching for the danger. Her eyes were starting to water and sting.

"Jade," Bennett said again, causing her to suddenly look at him. A horrified expression grew on her face.

"Oh," was all she could manage at first. It was barely above a whisper. She looked away from him and at the disheveled room. "Oh."

"Are you all right?" he asked.

A second later a tear slipped down her face. Another fell and she looked from Lewis, where he stood at the foot of the bed, to Bennett, where he sat beside her, and then down at her hands, which were trembling in her lap.

"I'm so sorry," she whispered, more tears slipping from her face. "I'm sorry. I didn't mean to—" her voice squeaked, cutting herself off. It was obvious to them that she had been having a nightmare. That it had spooked her something awful.

"Oh, honey," Lewis sighed, walking over to the other side of the bed and sitting down. Her shoulders jerked as she tried to keep herself from crying. "You have nothing to apologize for."

A small sob escaped her, and by instinct her hands flew up to cover her mouth. Lewis and Bennett looked at each other. Silently, they agreed upon something, and both gently moved and wrapped their arms around Jade. And she let herself cry, hard, as they sat there, and they held her.

XIV

Jade woke up alone the next morning. Sunlight was peeking in through small holes in the blinds, casting little yellow dots in a line across the room. She didn't dream again that night.

A feeling of shame suddenly overtook her as she looked around the room and saw the mess she'd made. The large wooden dresser sat diagonally, about two feet away from the wall. Bottles, trinkets, and picture frames were sprawled across the floor. Glass from the broken frames and the busted bulb glittered in the little patches of sun. Everything was either broken or out of place.

A lump formed in her throat, and she swallowed hard. Her eyes started to sting. She felt shame and embarrassment. And anger that she'd somehow allowed herself to do this. To let it happen again.

The first time something like this happened was during the second night after she'd been given the serum that made her this way. She'd been dreaming and was abruptly woken up by an ice-cold jet of water being shot at her with a hose. The second time it happened, she'd destroyed her living quarters. For that, she had to sleep hooked up to a machine for a month. That machine would record her brain waves as she slept, and when they started to show signs of her starting to use her telekinetic powers, it would send shocks through her body, waking her up before it could begin. She quickly learned to control her dreams after that.

But then she remembered how kind Lewis and Bennett had been. How they'd come to wake her up. But they didn't hurt her. They didn't punish her for it. They *comforted* her. And they waited until she had fallen asleep, until they knew she was ok, before they left her alone again. *And they barely know her.* The people from the Lab had known her for ten years, and they *tortured* her.

She closed her eyes and covered her face with her hands. She tried taking deep breaths. The tightness in her throat started to disappear, and her heart wasn't beating so hard. She breathed in deeply once more, and suddenly the smell of food filled her nose. Her hands fell away from her face, and she looked toward the bedroom door. She listened and thought she heard movement from somewhere else inside the house.

They must be awake, she thought, and slowly swung her legs over the edge of the bed. Her feet touched something soft, and she jerked them back up. She looked down and saw a pair of black slippers there, waiting. She instantly knew that one of them (it turned out to have been Lewis) had left them there for her because they didn't want her to step in the glass. The gesture made her want to cry again, but she kept her composure. She put them on her feet and shuffled over to the door, opening it quietly.

She walked down the hall and could hear movement in the kitchen. She could also hear someone humming. She could really smell the food now. It smelled sweet, but there was also something that vaguely smelled like smoke. She turned the corner and stood just outside of the open kitchen.

Lewis and Bennett were both standing in there—Lewis at the stove, turning something over in a pan, and Bennett humming as he waited for a pot of coffee to finish brewing. Bennett's hair was a little disheveled, making it obvious that he hadn't been awake for very long. She stood there silently for a moment, watching them. They seemed peaceful, just coexisting like that. She didn't want to disrupt it. Then Bennett turned around, pouring coffee into a mug, and saw her there. He smiled at her warmly. "Good morning, Jade."

Lewis looked over and smiled at her also, giving her a little wave, spatula still in hand.

"Morning," Lewis said. She returned their smiles shyly. She remembered the messy room and her expression faltered just for a second, before going back.

"Hi." She walked over to the counter and sat on one of the wooden stools. She watched as Bennett took the mug he'd just filled and placed it on the counter beside the stove, for Lewis. Then he grabbed another mug from the cabinet and started to fill it too. He glanced over at her.

"Would you like some?" He asked, offering the second filled coffee mug. She thought about it for a moment then finally shook her head.

"I'm ok."

"You sure? There's plenty."

"I'm sure." She nodded.

"Well, if you change your mind, let me know, and I'll make you a cup."

She nodded again. "Ok."

"Lewis is making pancakes," Bennett announced. "And he's frying up some of those canned sausages from the bomb shelter." He paused for a moment. "Do you like pancakes?" he asked.

Jade shrugged. "I don't know." She answered. "I don't think I've ever had pancakes."

Bennett squinted at her a little bit, then slowly started to nod his head. "I think you'll like pancakes." He finally said. His sudden declaration made her grin, and she laughed a little.

"But you don't have to eat them if you don't like them," Lewis said, turning around to face the two. "We're not going to force you to eat pancakes."

Bennett nodded enthusiastically. "Yes, of course," he said, but when Lewis turned around again, he leaned over closer to Jade and whispered: "But I still think you're going to like them. Lewis makes great pancakes." And it made her laugh even more.

Thomas O'Riley stood over the dead body of Michael Weston, which had been brought to the bomb shelter to be identified. Some of the team members working on

Protocol 42 were assigned to track down locations that the three targets may have gone to. So far, this was the first stop. And it was obvious that they'd been there. But how long they'd been there, and how long ago they'd left, remained a mystery. So did where they were going.

The black body bag that Michael was held in was zipped up and taken away. Thomas walked away from the entrance to the shelter and walked over to the vehicle, where a phone had someone on hold. He took it and answered it.

"So," Director Harris said on the other end of the line. "What have you found?"

"They've definitely been here," Thomas started. "But there's nothing here that tells us where they were going. Other than it must have been far, based on how much food is missing from inside."

"All right," the director said. "And the boy?"

"We found his body about a quarter mile from the shelter. Shot through the head."

"What a shame." Director Harris sighed. "I suppose that'll be all then, O'Riley. I'll have our boys start working to finish up the prep for the Protocol. Once we have a good idea of where they went, we'll move in on them as soon as possible."

"Yes, sir."

XV

Jade had insisted on cleaning the room herself. Bennett and Lewis had been on their way to do it after breakfast when she stopped them.

"It's my mess," she'd said. "You shouldn't have to clean it up." They had each tried to protest a little, saying they could at least help her do it. But they were doing enough for her as it was. They were already *in* her mess.

She now stood alone in the middle of the bedroom. Bennett had tried to give her the broom and dustpan, but she said she didn't need them. Just the trash can from the kitchen.

She started with the glass on the floor. She closed her eyes and took a deep breath, starting to concentrate on the shards scattered across the floor. She opened her eyes and the pieces started to move. They slid over the hardwood and began gathering into a pile. Then they each, piece by piece, started to rise into the air until there was a golf ball-sized mass of broken glass hovering four feet above the ground. She moved the trash can—without touching it—under the mass and slowly let the pieces fall. They cascaded down like a crystal rain, fragments of sunlight catching them as they fell, throwing dots of light across the room. She looked from the dresser to the bedside tables, and with a "push" had them all moving to their original positions. She walked over to the lamp and picked it up with her hands, placing it back in the corner.

"We've narrowed down two locations that Jade Cooper, along with Lewis and Bennett Hayes, could have gone," Director Harris started. He stood at the front of a large seminar room. The projector had a map thrown on the wall behind him. He hit a button on the remote in his hands and two red and two black circles appeared. The two black circles represented the Hayeses' cabin and the bomb shelter.

"Our first location is the last known residence of Mr. and Mr. Hayes." An arrow and label popped up onto the screen, pointing at the leftmost red circle. It was positioned forty miles northwest of the cabin.

"We have confirmed that the home has been vacant and on the market for three years." He pressed another button and another arrow and label appeared on the map just above the rightmost red circle. "The second location is the previous home of Bennett Hayes's deceased mother. This house has been vacant since the passing of Julia Hayes, five years ago.

"We will begin a search of the two properties tomorrow. Everyone assigned will need to be on the plane and heading out by 0800 hours. The plane is scheduled to land at 1130. From there, your respective teams will leave the airport in one of the two designated trucks. You will be taken to the hideout, and from there you will leave to your assigned location.

"Each team is to do an inspection of the property. You must remain unseen, by any means necessary, by our targets. If you are caught, it could jeopardize the entire operation. Stealth is your number one priority. This time of observation will determine which, if either, of the two properties our targets are occupying. Then, our team stationed at the Lab will be notified, and all individuals and prepared utilities will be immediately moved and positioned. We may only have one shot at this. Our main target is an extremely powerful individual. She may not look like it, but *you will not let your guard down*. As for the other two, they will be taken into custody and be dealt with accordingly. Are there any questions?"

Silence filled the room. Some of the listeners shook their heads, and others stared—a little scared—at the map still plastered up behind Director Harris. No one spoke.

"All right then. I would suggest you go ahead and pack your things immediately. And pack for a long trip."

Everyone started rising from their chairs and moving toward the exits. Thomas O'Riley remained seated in his chair at the front of the room until there was no one else but him and the director. He rose and walked over to where Director Harris was gathering papers and stacking them into a briefcase. He shut it just as Thomas reached him. He looked up.

"Oh, O'Riley," he said, clicking the locks together on the case before straightening himself and facing Thomas. "I was hoping I'd catch you before you'd gone." Thomas remained silent, waiting.

"I wanted to ask you if you'd like to oversee one of the two teams going to observe the properties. You're the only person I have who's seen this girl in the open. I think it would help the teams to have more than just a scientist or two tell them what to expect." He shoved his hands into his pants pockets. "I'll even let you have your pick of the property," he added with a grin.

Thomas hated that grin. He hated this *man*. But he wasn't going to pass on an opportunity like this, so he agreed.

"Excellent," Director Harris said, a gave a light slap to Thomas's good shoulder. The impact still sent a shooting pain through his injured one, and he fought back a grimace. "I won't keep you here any longer then. I know I still have a bit of packing to do, and I'm sure you do as well. Good luck with your observation, O'Riley. I look forward to hearing what you find."

Thomas watched the director as he walked across the seminar room, briefcase swinging at his side, toward the exit. He watched as Director Harris pushed open the door and kept watching even after he disappeared. He *hated* him. He didn't really know why he hated him, but he did.

Jade sat on the back patio, concentrating on the stream. She was stacking the rocks. Some weighed forty pounds, but it made no difference. She was stacking them with no particular order in mind. It was *good* to practice like this. It was *useful.* It allowed her to work on her concentration—which she didn't need much of, nowadays—when she wanted to move things. Making her use her skill was one of the only useful things that the people from the Lab did for her. It was constant use that allowed her to do things like dishevel an entire room in her sleep or lift 100 tons worth of metal. She knew she needed to use it more if she was going to face the Lab again—which she knew she would, eventually.

She had the stack up to ten feet when Lewis opened the back door and stepped out onto the porch. The stack didn't falter as she turned her head to look at him. She gave him a small smile, which he immediately returned.

"Hi."

"Hey."

He shoved his hands into his jeans pockets as he made his way over to the bench.

"Whatcha doin'?" he asked as he took a seat beside her.

A light blush crept to her cheeks, and she became a little embarrassed. "Practicing," she answered, and gestured over to the tower of rocks.

Lewis wasn't surprised to see it there. He'd already caught a glimpse of what she was doing through the kitchen window. He nodded, and they sat quietly for a few moments, listening to the woods around them.

"How are you doing?" he asked, and the tower made a scraping noise but quickly stilled before any of the rocks fell. He watched them move slightly, righting themselves.

"I'm ok," she answered, but she didn't look at him. Her eyes were now glued to the rock formation. He knew she was lying.

"You sure?" he prodded. "Because it's all right if you're not. Ok, I mean. It's ok if you're not ok." She didn't answer. "You're allowed to not be ok all the time."

She started to pick at the skin around her nails, and with a slight scraping sound the rocks were slowly being removed from the stack and placed into the stream again.

"No. I guess I'm not ok," she finally admitted, still not looking at him. But it was a start. And he'd take what he could get.

"That's understandable." He nodded, leaning forward and putting his elbows on his knees. He watched the rocks as they moved through the air and disappeared into the water. He figured it'd make her more comfortable, and willing to talk, if neither of them was looking at the other. "You've been through a lot. These last couple days have been wild; not to mention the things that happened before."

A knot formed in her stomach. She continued to pick at her hands. The rocks slowed until it was hard to tell they were moving at all until they'd made significant progress downward.

"What's troubling you?"

She looked at him briefly, and a light scoff escaped her. "What isn't troubling me is a better question." Lewis's eyebrows raised momentarily, and he nodded, letting out a slightly embarrassed chuckle.

"Start with something small, then."

She thought for a moment. "I don't have any pictures," she whispered. Lewis was confused by the somewhat random statement, but he didn't let it show on his face. He waited patiently for her to continue.

"I don't have any memories from before I was taken by the Lab. Anything that I may have said, experienced, friends I might have had...they're all gone. Wiped from memory." She paused. The rock she had just been moving stopped and hovered in the air for what felt like a long time. It dropped with a small splash into the water. "Part of me thinks that it was all the experiments. That it was all the serums that they injected me with that affected my memories somehow. But I also think I made myself forget, because remembering what I had before would have been too painful." She looked over at him, tears brimming in her eyes. "I wasn't wanted. No one cared that I was there. *But I was free.* I was ignored, but I wasn't *tortured.*" A tear slipped down her face, and she made no move to wipe it away. She simply looked away from him, back to the stream. The rock formation continued its undoing.

A lump had formed in Lewis's throat, and his chest felt like it was filled with the very stones from the stream. But he didn't say anything. Because sometimes people just need to be listened to. They don't always need feedback to feel heard.

"I'm also afraid of what will happen when they find me," she started again. "When they find *us*. It's only a matter of time before they do." Her hands were shaking, but her fingers never stopped picking. "I don't really know what to expect."

"I'm pretty scared too," Lewis said. She looked at him and he gave her a sad smile. "But not for me. I'm scared for you; for *your* future." He paused and sat up. "You deserve much more good than you've been given."

Another tear slipped down her face, and she retreated her gaze to her lap. Her hands stilled. Her throat felt tight, and her chest burned as she tried to keep herself from crying any harder. She'd cried a lot in the last few days. "Thanks."

Lewis hesitated before speaking again. "I can't pretend and say something like 'I know what you're going through,' or 'I know how you feel.' But I can offer my ears if you ever need them." He shrugged his shoulders. "And if you don't want to say anything, if you just want to sit quietly, and have someone be there so you're not alone, I can offer my company."

Jade's heart hurt. But it wasn't a bad kind of hurt. It was a new kind of pain. She smiled at him through her tears.

"Thank you, Lewis."

He smiled warmly at her in return and placed a hand on her shoulder, giving it a light squeeze.

XVI

The uneven road had Thomas constantly knocking his shoulder into the vehicle door. It was a thirty-minute drive from the hideout to the camp that was set up a mile from the late mother's house; and with five minutes left, Thomas was dying for the trip to end. His shoulder was throbbing. Zaps of pain shot up his neck and down his arm with every other bump in the road.

Thomas had picked Bennett Hayes's dead mother's house based on a gut feeling. The other house seemed irrelevant to him for some reason. Besides, it was twice the distance away from the cabin. He didn't think the three of them—if the three of them were even still together—would have walked that far. And he was sure that, even if they found only Lewis and Bennett at first, they could get it out of them where she was heading. It really wasn't that hard to get people to talk. Especially when they feared for their lives. Or the life of someone they cared about.

The camp was completely set up when they finally arrived. The trailers were all positioned in a large circle; the trucks all faced outward, ready to leave in a hurry if need be. There was a group of fifteen men and women standing in wait in the middle of the camp. Thomas practically jumped out of the truck to meet them, not wanting to be in the vehicle for a second longer than he needed to be. He wanted to get this over with. The introductions, the planning. By 0600 tomorrow morning, they would all need to be in their positions on the property and beginning the investigation.

"Good afternoon, everyone. My name is Officer Thomas O'Riley. You should all already have a clear goal in mind, and that goal is to confirm the location of our target, Jade Cooper." He paused to look at them all. They looked serious enough about the whole thing. And he was sure that some of them had even done observations like this before. But not with targets like this one. They're all used to regular human beings. Jade was not that.

"As you all know, Jade Cooper is an escaped subject of the Lab. She was one of the subjects being transferred on November 13. What some—if not most—of you probably don't know, is that that particular transfer contained the most powerful individuals to be produced by the Lab.

"I know that scientists from the Lab have informed you all about her Telekinetic abilities, but they have only ever seen her in controlled, experimental environments. I have seen her crush things without hardly moving a muscle. I've seen her lift 100 tons ten feet off the ground. There is no known limit to what she can do with this ability. And because of this, I need each and every one of you to *always* be on high alert during your observation duties. Hesitation will be the thing that kills you when it comes down to it."

Some of their faces paled; others were sweating from nervousness. This was good. They needed to *feel* how serious this operation was. How important the *success* of this operation was. Because for all they knew, Jade could conquer the world.

"I'd like to start by discussing positions around the property, and how to properly switch shifts. The confirming process might take two hours, two days, or two weeks. However long it'll take, you need to be prepared.

"Once the confirmation is made, if there is one to be made, you will radio back to camp and tell them of your findings *before* you leave your posts. We don't have time to chase false information. Is that understood?"

They all nodded.

"Great. Let's get going then, shall we?"

The sun was just beginning to lighten when Thomas arrived at his post the next morning. He was positioned so that he could see the entirety of the back patio. The blinds on all the windows were drawn, but there was nothing covering the sliding glass door, which made it easier to see inside. There were three other teams set up around the house: one at the front of the house and one on either side of the house. They needed to make sure there were no exits left unattended.

A lone bird started to sing in the distance. Thomas pressed a button on the handheld radio—which was hooked up to an earpiece—that connected him to each post.

"Everyone keep your eyes peeled. You see anything—anything at all—you radio it in."

"Copy that."

"Copy."

"We read ya loud and clear, boss."

Boss. Thomas liked the sound of that.

Nothing happened for the first two hours. The only movement or sound came from the forest around them. The radio suddenly let out a soft squeak.

"I've got movement in the front room. Appears to be only one figure walking around. I'll keep you posted."

At the same time Thomas saw a shadow walk by the back door.

"Affirmative. I can confirm, there is movement inside the house," he answered. He watched the doors intently for a few minutes but did not see the figure walk past again. A minute or two later, light gray smoke started to rise from the chimney, quickly turning black as it continued to burn. *Whoever's in there must be comfortable*, he thought. *No way it's some squatter if they're brave enough to build a fire*. He pressed the button again.

"Eyes open, everyone."

Thomas's heart skipped a beat when a figure from inside of the house pushed open the sliding glass door and stepped out onto the porch. It was now well past noon. He, and everyone else, had been sitting, watching, and waiting for nine hours.

And here she was. She wore black sweatpants that were way too baggy, black socks, and a light gray sweatshirt. It was weird, seeing her in anything but the clothes from the Lab. She almost looked like a *person* to Thomas. Brief flashes of the gun crumpling in his hands, and the exploding, floating trucks took that thought and chucked it into the sun. He pressed the button on his radio.

"I can confirm that our target is on the property," he said in a low voice. He knew that there was no way that she could hear him, even if he spoke at a normal volume, from this distance. But a big part of him was still afraid of the off chance that she already knew he was there, that she knew they were *all* there, watching her. A crackle in his earpiece sent a shiver down his spine. He pressed the button again, hand slightly shaking. "Jade Cooper has just stepped out onto the back patio."

"Copy that," came the voice of the woman watching the front of the house. "What is our next move, Officer O'Riley?"

"Two teams will remain on the property, and the other two will return to base camp and relay our findings." Point A was positioned at the front of the house, point B at the back of the house, point C on the left side, and point D on the right side. "Once Ms. Brady and I return to camp, I will send two new observers to take your places, and they will continue the rotation. *Do not*, under any circumstances, *leave this property*."

"Understood."

"Yes, sir."

With that, Thomas waited for Ms. Brady to reach his location before they walked the half mile or so back to the truck that was waiting for them.

O'Riley went to the phone the second they returned and dialed the number for the hideout. He had to go through three secretaries before he finally got ahold of Director Harris.

"Hello?"

"Director Harris, this is Officer O'Riley."

"Ah, O'Riley, good to hear it. How are things going at the Julia Hayes location?"

"Well, sir, we found her."

There was silence on the other end of the line. Static rose to a deafening volume as he waited for Director Harris's response.

"Are you sure?" His voice was low, just like how Thomas's was at his post. Like he was afraid that somehow Jade knew.

"Yes, sir. I was the one who identified her. I watched her exit the house from the back door onto the porch."

There was more silence.

In his office in the hideout, Director Harris's heart felt like it had slowed. He could feel each individual spasm. His chest hurt. He felt dizzy. He was having trouble thinking.

"I'll notify everyone immediately," he finally said. His voice sounded far away from him. "By 1900 hours we will have everything for Protocol 42 moved from the hideout to the camp. By 0300 hours the next morning, everything will be moved to the property and set up posthaste."

"Yes, sir. I'll be here waiting."

"Good, good. I will call the camp when the equipment and I are on our way."

"Understood." And they hung up the phone.

Director Harris never called the camp again. Two hours after notifying everyone that the target had been found, and that the transport of the equipment for Protocol 42 was to be set into motion, Joshua Harris was found in his office by his secretary Jackie. He'd had a heart attack and was pronounced dead on the scene.

XVII

"Seems like the guy is bad luck to me," Agent Black said to the very small group around him. They were waiting for the arrival of the equipment from the hideout. They'd all just heard about Director Harris's death. He took a sip of the quickly cooling coffee in his hands.

"You really shouldn't say things like that," Ms. Brady said from beside him. Two others nodded, but the rest stayed motionless.

"Why not? I mean think about it," Black started again. "There was the incident that led to the escape of the target, Jade Cooper. Eight of our men and three subjects were killed that night. Then there was the cabin incident, which killed more of our men—one of whom was his partner, James White. And now Director Harris. And who was there for all three of those events?"

Everyone remained silent. They didn't want to believe that the man in charge of this operation was, in fact, bad luck. But it was getting a little hard not to think about it. Right now, Thomas O'Riley was instructing everyone else on what to do when the delivery arrived.

"I'm just saying," Black began again after a long moment of silence. "I wouldn't be surprised if more of us end up dead in the near future."

The moment Jade had stepped out onto the porch, her skin had turned into goose flesh; the hairs on her arms and the back of her neck stood on end. It caught her off guard, but she tried to ignore it. She went over to the bench and took a seat. She'd come out with the intention of enjoying the day—sitting out in the sun, listening to the nature around her. It was something she never got to do in the Lab. And she wasn't sure how long she'd be able to until they showed up again. She wanted to savor the few moments she had. But the feeling that something was *wrong* created knots in her stomach. Her heart was pounding, even though it wasn't beating quickly. She stayed out there as long as she could—which only ended up being about ten minutes—before she went inside.

Lewis and Bennett were standing in the kitchen talking when she reentered the house. Their conversation stopped, and they looked at her. They both grew concerned rather quickly. They hadn't expected her to be out there for such a short amount of time. And the expression on her face was deeply troubled.

"Are you all right?" Lewis asked. Bennett set down the cup in his hand. She didn't respond. She just stood there, quietly, looking down at the floor. Her eyes shifted back and forth across the hardwood, but not like they were seeing anything. More like she was thinking, like her mind was racing.

"Jade?" Bennett said, taking a small step toward her. Her head lifted slowly, and she looked at them.

"I'm sorry," she said softly. "I'm not sure what's going on."

Anxiety began building in Lewis's and Bennett's stomachs. They glanced at each other briefly.

"What?"

"What are you talking about?" They spoke in unison. Jade's brows furrowed and her hands subconsciously rose to her chest, her fingers intertwining. The hairs on her skin still stood, making her skin feel prickly, almost electrified.

"Something's not right," she said. Her eyes seemed to be looking through them. Unbeknownst to her, she was looking in the exact direction of point C. "Something's not right," she repeated.

At the camp, new trucks from the hideout were arriving. Each truck had three huge crates filled with the force field devices designed for Protocol 42.

At exactly 3:00 in the morning, the large, boxy devices were being placed around the four-acre property in a circle. The devices were positioned twenty feet from each other all the way around. They gave off a low humming noise once the switches were flipped and they were turned on. The field wouldn't start to form until everyone was positioned inside of the circle. Once that had been accomplished, a button would be pressed just outside of the barrier, and up the field would go.

XVIII

Jade got no sleep that night. She spent most of the night pacing around the room, sometimes venturing out to the living room if she got too claustrophobic. The prickly feeling all over her skin and the knot in her stomach never went away. Any time she tried to sleep, a piece of furniture would move. The constant sound of Jade moving around—not to mention the occasional scrape of a dresser or nightstand sliding across the floor—made it no easier for Lewis and Bennett to sleep either. Lewis turned over so that the two were facing each other.

"If you could be any animal, what would you be?" Lewis whispered.

"What?" Bennett chuckled lightly. "Why are you asking me this?"

"I don't know," Lewis replied, shrugging his shoulders. "Just trying to pass the time, I guess."

Bennett laughed again; the smile not leaving his face as he thought about the question. "I guess I'd be a Saint Bernard."

"Yeah? How come?"

"Well, I guess 'cause Saint Bernards are kind of intimidating to look at, 'cause they're such big dogs. But under all that fluff they're just gentle giants."

Lewis smiled and they both laughed. "Yeah, I guess that makes sense."

"What about you? What would you be?"

Lewis thought about it for a minute. "I think I'd *want* to be a lion, or a tiger. Something big and strong and scary. But I know deep down I'm just a house cat," he answered, which sent Bennett into a loud burst of laughter.

Lewis shushed him, failing to contain his own laughs.

"Ok, ok," Bennett sighed, trying to stop his laughter. "If you could relive any moment from your life, what would it be and why?"

Lewis whistled and turned onto his back. "Damn," he said, looking over at Bennett. "That's a good one."

Bennett grinned and nodded his head. "Oh, I know. Now answer."

"Well," Lewis began, still thinking. "I think meeting you for the first time again would be pretty cool."

A dumbstruck expression plastered itself onto Bennett's face, and his mouth hung agape. He propped himself up on one elbow so that he could look down at Lewis.

"That's not fair," he said, aghast. "That was my answer!"

Lewis rolled his eyes and shook his head. "Yeah, yeah, whatever," he said with a grin. "You just wanted to copy me so I'd like you more."

Bennett gave his husband a mock frown and plopped himself back down onto his side.

"So what made you say you'd want to meet me again?" Bennett asked, a small smile on his face.

Lewis looked at him for a long moment before answering. "Because you weren't even supposed to be there," Lewis started, a grin spreading across his face as he recalled the memory. "You were invited to that party at the last minute, and you showed up. And you completely caught me off guard." He turned to his side, so they were facing each other again. "You were this beaming source of light and kindness. There was simply no way you were getting rid of me," he finished, which made them both laugh.

"Oh, come on, we both know I was the clingy one." Bennett giggled.

Lewis rolled his eyes and gave Bennett a soft shove. They suddenly heard a thunk in one of the other rooms and were yanked back to reality.

Bennett sighed, and a sad smile appeared on his face. "Poor kid."

"I know."

"I just wish there was something we could do, you know? I mean, I know that were doing what we can. But I just wish there was…*more*."

Lewis grabbed both of Bennett's hands and gave them a light squeeze.

"Me too, Benny. Me too."

PART TWO

Inexorable

(adj.) impossible to stop; unchangeable; inevitable

I

It was very early in the morning when the small battalion started for the house. Four cruisers and eight heavily armored trucks carrying ten men each moved through the forest toward the edge of the property. Each man was heavily armored and carried specialized weapons in hand: dart guns that were modified by the Lab to fit darts filled with the same serum as the one that was embedded in Michael's collar—the one that allowed them to control him. Of course, they had real guns on their persons too, but those were to be used only as a last resort. The Lab wanted her alive at all costs.

"We need to get out of here."

The three stood—Jade just outside of Lewis and Bennett's room in the hall, and the couple just inside the door frame. They had been woken up by Jade knocking on their door. They were both half-awake but could feel the tension that seeped from her. She was shifting her weight from side to side; her hands were working at each other. As she stood there, waiting for an answer, her gaze constantly shifted between the two men before her and the end of the hall. Her eyes were pleading every time they came back to Lewis and Bennett.

"Please," she said. "We need to go."

"What's this about?" Bennett asked, rubbing his eyes with his hands. "What's wrong?"

"I don't—I don't know, ok? But I've been up all night, and I can't shake this feeling that something is really, *really* wrong." Fright-filled tears were building in her eyes, and her throat felt like it was getting tighter. Her chest burned, and her hands were starting to shake. A tear slipped. "Please?"

"Ok," Lewis said from where he stood, slightly behind Bennett. He came forward and held both of her shoulders with a reassuring firmness. "Go and make sure your things are together, ok?"

She nodded and hurried down the hall, disappearing into her room.

Lewis pulled Bennett back into their room and closed the door behind them.

"What is going *on*?" Bennett asked, still groggy from sleep.

Lewis walked across the room, not looking at him. "I don't know," he said as he grabbed his backpack off the ground and started shoving his things into it. "But I trust her intuition a lot more than I trust ours."

Bennett had just started to make his way over to where his own bag was when the sound started. It was a low, droning noise that sounded like an ominous, broken siren. Everyone in the house froze.

The sound dragged on for a minute and a half before suddenly switching into a dull ringing that very much resembled the sensation of tinnitus. Smooth skin turned to goose flesh. Lewis and Bennett looked at each other, eyes wide and terrified. Jade stood in the middle of her room, alone.

The force field around the property had just gone up.

A long squeaking noise, like feedback from a microphone, cut through the air like a knife, then stopped as suddenly as it had started. And then a voice came and sent a shiver down Jade's spine.

"We have the house surrounded. Do not attempt escape," the amplified voice said. Jade could hear her heartbeat in her ears. Her hands were shaking even worse now. "Jade," the voice started again. Tears filled her eyes. "We know you're in there."

Outside, Thomas lowered the megaphone so it was hanging at his side. Surrounding him and the house were the many armored men. He stood at the back of the house, thirty feet away from the porch.

When she finally did exit the house, the air around them suddenly felt like it was vibrating. Tension rose to its peak, and immediately the modified weapons were raised and aimed at her. Lewis and Bennett came out just behind her. None of the three brought anything outside. There wasn't any point.

Thomas's heart rate quickened at the sight of her there, on the porch. *So close. And trapped.* There was nowhere for her to go, and he knew it. He was sure she knew it too. He could *feel* it, and it made him almost giddy. He smiled at her.

"What a pleasure it is to see you again, Ms. Cooper," he called, obvious sarcasm in his voice. He shifted his weight to one side. "A shame that it had to be like this, though."

The buzzing feeling intensified. Bennett grabbed Lewis's hand and squeezed it. Just the sight of it all—*the effort*—that these people obviously went through to get to her, it...well, quite simply, it petrified them. It horrified them for themselves, for each other...and for her.

"There are two ways that all this might go, but either way, you *will* be coming with us, Jade. You can either come peacefully and bring yourself on down those steps, let my men put the cuffs on you, and hop into one of these trucks. Or you can try to fight us. But you won't get very far." He turned in a half circle, looking around at the people surrounding the house. His head tilted back to look up to the sky, where he could see the shimmer of the force field over the sun. "Even if you manage to get past my men here, there's still a barrier around the entire property." His eyes moved from Jade to Lewis and Bennett. He stared at them for a moment, before slowly returning to Jade. "And I'm sure you don't want anything to happen to your new friends here, do you? I'd be a real shame if they got hurt because you couldn't do as you were told."

The moment the threat left his mouth, a few of the armored men who held regular guns shifted their aim to Lewis and Bennett. Bennett squeezed his eyes shut and let out a shaky exhale. Lewis's grip on his hand tightened even more. He wanted to lean over to Bennett, tell him soothing things, but he didn't dare move. And he didn't want to risk lying to him by saying something like "We'll be all right."

Jade's eyes scanned across every face that surrounded the back of the house. She started with the ones aiming their weapons at the two men behind her. Then the ones aiming at her. She watched as some of their composures faltered slightly, just by her looking at them. On the outside, she looked completely unbothered, which scared them. Her eyes went back to Officer O'Riley.

The tension was almost deafening. Everyone's skin crawled with anticipation.

"So, what'll it be, Jade?" There was silence for a long moment.

"I'll come," Jade started. The sudden sound of her voice sent shivers down spines. "But you need to promise me that nothing is going to happen to them," she finished.

She didn't move, didn't gesture in any way toward Lewis and Bennett, but Thomas knew what she meant. He grinned at her. "Sure," he said with a slight shrug. She narrowed her eyes at him, and a flurry of anxious moths rippled in the pit of his stomach.

"Swear it," she demanded, her voice dark. She was no longer worried about what happened to *her*. The men behind her—the men who had shown her kindness, and a thing kind of like love—were all that mattered to her now. For them, she could be fearless—or at least pretend to be as best she could. Thomas let out a scoff and held his arms behind his back.

"I swear," he said, all the while crossing his fingers like a child. The buzzing in the air stopped abruptly. The sudden stillness sent more shivers down all their spines.

What sounded like a loud, metallic creaking filled the silence while Jade moved to take a step toward the porch stairs. In that instant, panic filled the men carrying the dart guns and fingers squeezed triggers. Jade's eyes widened as she watched, almost in slow motion, as the darts came flying at her. She struggled to catch them before they reached her; before the needles plunged into her skin. But she was rushed. While eleven darts hung unmoving in the air, six others bit into her flesh.

The serums were administered immediately when the needles were stuck in skin. And their effects started just as fast. The suspended darts fell to the floor with multiple *clinking* sounds as Jade's body began to convulse. Her knees buckled, and she crumpled onto the porch.

"Jade!" Lewis and Bennett both screamed, rushing to her. They landed roughly on their knees, one on either side of her. She could feel them both around her. Lewis held both of her hands in his own, and Bennett held her head in his lap, trying to keep her from slamming her head into the wooden deck.

"It's ok, you're gonna be ok," Lewis said shakily. Frightened tears were building in his eyes. Streams of them were already falling down Bennett's face. These were the last things Jade heard and saw before her eyes rolled back and there was nothing.

When her body finally stilled, Lewis and Bennett held their breaths. Their hearts sank when her eyes opened. Her brown eyes were replaced by black pits with a small, white dot where her pupils should have been. And they knew it was done. That she was gone. Locked away. This wasn't Jade anymore. Jade was somewhere else.

From where he stood, Thomas sighed, and with a lazy wave of his hand, men rushed the porch. Neither Lewis nor Bennett fought as they were pulled away from Jade. They didn't resist when their hands were cuffed behind their backs and they were escorted to the back of a cruiser.

From inside the car, they watched as Jade stood robotically and walked down the steps, across the yard, and into the back of one of the large, armored trucks. They looked at each other then, as she disappeared from their sight.

II

She woke in a pool of her own sweat. Her skin was cold with it, and her head throbbed. She rubbed her eyes with the backs of her hands. The room was dim, lit only by a single dull lightbulb overhead. The bed beneath her was hard.

Her heartbeat quickened as she very quickly recognized the room. She scrambled backward until her back roughly hit the concrete wall behind her. Her breathing was shallow and fast as her eyes darted back and forth across her old "bedroom."

Jade couldn't remember anything that had happened three days ago, when she was caught. Not yet anyway. That serum tended to cause temporary memory loss. She had been asleep since then, waking very seldomly, but not fully. She had wavered between consciousness and unconsciousness, never opening her eyes, muttering strange, incoherent sentences that puzzled the Lab workers.

She was suddenly very aware of the heavy metal collar around her neck, and the way her clothes felt on her skin. It was only now that she realized she was wearing not the borrowed clothes from Lewis and Bennett, but the clothes of the Lab.

Lewis and Bennett! She thought suddenly, eyes going wide. *Where are they?! What happened?!*

The door to the room opened and Jade almost jumped out of her skin. A woman entered, wearing a long white coat and holding a clipboard at her hip. Jade did not recognize her.

"Good afternoon, Jade," the woman said, quickly glancing at the clipboard before securing her gaze on the girl. As the door was closing, Jade caught a glimpse of four or five men waiting in the hall, each wearing protective gear and holding a gun. "How are you feeling today?"

Jade did not answer. Instead, she stared at the woman in front of her. The woman sighed.

"No," Jade mumbled. "No, no, no. This can't be happening." A sudden sharp pain erupted in her temples. She gritted her teeth and squeezed her eyes shut as her hands rose to each side of her head. A flashing image of her standing on the porch surrounded by Thomas and his men ripped through her mind. But nothing more. The pain in her head subsided. She opened her eyes slowly, staring at the floor at the doctor's feet. She knew it was one of her missing memories, but she didn't want to believe it. She wanted to believe that she could squeeze her eyes shut again, until her brain started to tingle, and then open them to reveal that she was still in that house, with Lewis and Bennett, and this was all just a bad dream.

The woman's expression softened a little as she watched Jade. She sighed. "Well, my dear, I've come to take you to your new quarters," she explained, placing her free hand into her coat pocket. Inside was a small remote. If she needed to—if Jade decided that she was going to be trouble—Dr. Waters could press a button, and the mind control serums embedded in her collar would be administered. She didn't think she'd need to use it, but she was a little more comfortable with it in her hand. "It's much more comfortable than this. You'll have a proper bed, your own private bathroom, and some other things to make it a bit more…well, homey." She looked around the dim, concrete room. *Well, about as homey as they could make a place like this,* she thought.

Jade sat motionless for a few moments before finally standing from the bed. She was a bit taller than Dr. Waters had expected. She'd looked so small all balled up in the corner. But Jade never looked at her. Never stole a glance. Some of her hair hung in her face, and she looked down at the floor beneath their feet. This made Dr. Waters nervous, but she didn't think she'd prefer it if Jade were looking at her, making eye contact. She knew that would have felt more ominous than the shadows that covered Jade's face.

But Jade wasn't trying to be intimidating, or mysterious. Her mind was elsewhere. She was worrying about Lewis and Bennett, who, unbeknownst to her, were sitting in a room just a few doors down the hall.

III

Jade sat on the edge of her new bed, looking around the new room. The first thing she noticed was the bathroom. The door was slightly open, and the fact that it had a door to begin with had shocked her. There was no lock, but she was grateful for the little bit of privacy they were granting her.

The next thing she had noticed was that all the furniture was welded to the floor: the bed frame, the bedside table, and the big round table with three chairs that sat on the far left side of the room. Pretty much anything that was big and could move was fused to the ground.

And finally, the window. It wasn't a very big window, but she could see the world outside if she got up on her tiptoes. Well, she could see the giant field filled with trees behind the Lab, at least.

It was overwhelming. The Lab had never given her any kind of human courtesy before. And now she had a private bathroom? And a *window*? Something wasn't right. They needed her for something.

She was scared to find out what it was.

Lewis and Bennett sat silently as they waited. They sat in a room much like Jade's. Except everything was moveable. And they had no window.

The couple sat side-by-side on the queen-size bed. Their hands were tangled together, and Lewis's head rested on Bennett's shoulder, Bennett's head on top of Lewis's. They were very tired. Neither of them had slept much in the past three days. Constantly they were being interrogated by the Lab workers. They were being asked questions—all that strangely had nothing to do with Jade or why they were there—and the Lab workers were writing things down on their clipboards. Any time Lewis or Bennett would try asking about Jade, the Lab workers would immediately stop what they were doing and leave the room. But the couple never stopped asking.

There was a small knock on the main door, and both of their heads rose. It opened with a loud creak, and Dr. Waters stepped in. She, like everyone else who'd been in there to talk to them, wore a white lab coat and held a clipboard at her hip.

"Good afternoon, gentlemen," she greeted them. "My name is Dr. Waters." She walked over to the big round table and pulled out one of the chairs but did not sit down. She stood, looking at them with a pleasant expression on her face. She waited patiently for the two to stand from where they sat and walk the eight or so feet it took for them to reach the table. She laid down her clipboard—face down—and took her seat. Lewis and Bennett sat opposite of her.

It was important for her to take a mental note of the fact that there were no cameras in the room. In Jade's room, yes. But not this one. They had bugged this one instead. So anything that they—or she—said would be recorded for anyone to hear. She folded her hands on the table and gave the men before her a soft smile.

"I can imagine that this must all be a bit, well, frightening," she started, mindlessly reaching for her clipboard and flipping a few pages. "But I am here to hopefully put some of those fears to rest." She stopped flipping through the pages and, very silently, held up a loose sheet for them to see.

Do not bring up Jade first was written in neat handwriting across the blank white sheet. Lewis's and Bennett's hearts skipped. Their eyes widened, and they immediately looked at each other. Before they could say a word, Dr. Waters had a new sheet held up for them to read. The new page read: *The moment you say her name, I am forced to leave. You need me here.*

The couple sat still for a long moment before both nodded in understanding. She smiled at them and silently mouthed, "Good."

"Now, I understand you both have your concerns, and I am willing to answer any questions you might have to the best of my abilities." She started flipping through the pages again.

"How long are we going to be kept here?" Bennett asked. He hadn't wanted to speak, but it was the second thing on his mind after Jade, and he figured it was a safe question. She nodded at him, almost confirming this thought.

"Well, unfortunately, I don't exactly have a timeline for you," she began. She found a new page and spoke again before she held it up for them. "You both potentially have some very incriminating information about this organization." She held up the paper. "Because of that, we need to find out exactly what you know in order to figure out how to deal with you properly."

She's alive. But they have plans for her that may change that soon, the new page read.

Lewis cringed at the new piece of writing. Bennett visibly paled. He grabbed Lewis's hand under the table and squeezed it to regulate himself. Lewis was grateful for the contact.

"And how is that going to work?" Lewis asked so Bennett didn't have to find his voice again right away. Dr. Waters put the page back into the stack.

"Quite simply, really. I will come to see you every day, around the same time, and we will talk. I will ask you questions about your time with Jade Cooper, and you will answer truthfully. You will tell me everything that she said, and everything that she did. How long that takes is up to you." She sat quietly for a moment after she finished and watched the two men before her. She saw the fear still clear in their faces. But now there was a little bit of hope in there—guarded hope, but hope all the same. She took one last piece of paper from her clipboard and folded it silently. She slid it across the table but did not remove her hand. They both looked at her, questioningly.

"Does that sound like a plan?" she asked and removed her hand. Slowly, Lewis reached for the folded paper, and opened it for Bennett and himself to read.

I'm going to get you out of here, but I need you to do exactly as I tell you. Do you understand?

"Okay," Lewis said in a near whisper. She smiled warmly at them again and stood from her chair.

"Wonderful," she said, picking up her clipboard and gently taking the piece of paper from Lewis's hands. "I will see you both tomorrow then."

IV

She was sitting in the chair, and it made her sick to her stomach. *The* chair. The one with the wrist and ankle restraints. The one they used when they were about to test some new serum on her.

She hadn't been sleeping well, and she knew that was why she was here. It had to be. She must have been moving things around in her sleep. She'd been tossing and turning all night, some of her lost memories coming to her as dreams. Each one of them ended with a view of Thomas O'Riley standing in front of her, holding that stupid megaphone at his side, with a satisfied grin on his face. She *hated* him.

She then remembered that everything that had the potential to move in her room was welded to the floor, and she grew a little confused. *I couldn't have been moving things*, she thought. Her brows furrowed, and she absent-mindedly shifted around in the chair. She was starting to feel claustrophobic, from both the restraints and her racing thoughts. Her train of thought was beginning to spiral when the door to the big white room opened.

It was that woman from the day before, the one who'd taken her to the new room. The woman smiled at her as someone else closed the door behind her. It was only the two of them in the room. On the other side of the big mirror wall, three other Lab workers, along with seven guards, watched and recorded the interactions as they took place. The Lab workers were collecting data from the EEG and EKG machines that were hooked up to Jade. It was very important for their studies to be able to see the effects that the serums and the abilities they granted had on the heart and brain—especially with a subject such as Jade, whose given abilities were controlled by the mind. Also, it could be a little expensive to replace the test subjects. They needed to know if they were about to die before it was too late.

"Good morning, Jade," Dr. Waters addressed her.

Jade didn't respond. Instead, she watched the woman as she grabbed one of the rolling chairs positioned in the corner of the room and dragged it over. She sat down so that she was right in front of Jade. They were about a foot away from each other.

"I want to first apologize for such an early start to your day," the doctor began. "But Dr. Peters has instructed us to begin with your procedures as soon as we were able." She smiled at Jade again, but there was something wrong with it. It didn't reach her eyes, which looked sad in a way. A knot formed in Jade's stomach.

"Procedures?" she whispered.

If Dr. Waters hadn't been sitting so close to her, she never would have heard what Jade said. She was a little shocked, truth be told, that Jade had even spoken at all. She had been almost sure that she would be receiving the silent treatment from Jade for as long as she was to know her. The sadness in her eyes spread across her face for a quick second before disappearing. It made Jade's heart speed up.

"Yes," the doctor sighed. "Dr. Peters has much planned for you. Unfortunately, I am unable to tell you what those things are. But what I can say is that it shouldn't be too much worse than the things you've already been through."

That statement gave no relief or consolation to Jade, and it showed very clearly on her face. Her eyes started to sting, and her throat tightened.

I'm going to die here, she thought as she fought the tears that were building in her eyes. *They're going to use me up until there is nothing left for them to take, and then I'm going to die.*

Her eyes slowly drifted away from Dr. Waters, and a rogue tear slipped down her face. Her body felt like lead, and she slumped in the chair. "Do what you have to do, then," she said, and she did not speak again. Dr. Waters nodded and stood from the chair. Her head turned to look at the mirror wall, and she gestured to the people on the other side that it was their turn with Jade.

The door opened, and Dr. Waters made way for the young man who was pushing in a cart loaded with vials of the TK9 serum. This was the one that gave Jade her telekinetic abilities. The Lab had been making alterations to the serum long before her escape, and they were ready to test it. Their hope was that it would help unlock the full potential of her brain in using telekinesis or, at the very least, increase her strength. As silly as it sounds, they did know the risks. At all times, whether she was in this room, her own room, or the room designed for her to practice using her abilities, she was to wear the metal collar that held the mind control serums. If she were to suddenly decide to attack anyone, or attempt escape, a simple push of a button would administer the serums, and she would have no power over herself.

Dr. Waters stayed only long enough to watch the first needle sink into Jade's throat. She left quickly and started walking toward the elevator at the end of the hall. She pressed the button and waited a few moments before the doors opened, and she stepped inside. She pressed another button that would take her up to the sixth floor. The moment the doors closed, she sighed deeply. A weight had formed in her chest. She'd only gone up one floor when the elevator dinged and the doors opened again. In walked Thomas O'Riley. He entered and pressed the button for the tenth floor without ever acknowledging her.

His very presence was unnerving. There was a coldness to him that sent an actual shiver down Dr. Waters's spine. She had never met him before, but she knew exactly who he was. After the untimely death of the former director, Joshua Harris, Thomas O'Riley was appointed to the position by Dr. Peters himself. A memo was sent out to all Lab personnel saying that all were to respect and follow orders from Director O'Riley in Dr. Peters's absence. It was Thomas who'd sent out the instruction for Dr. Waters and her team to start the procedures on Jade this morning.

"Good morning, Director," Dr. Waters greeted him as they passed the third floor.

He looked at her, finally, with a reproachful eye. Then there was a hint of recognition in his expression. "Waters, isn't it?" he asked.

She nodded. "Yes, sir. Dr. Ruth Waters." She stuck her hand out for him to shake.

He seemed almost taken aback by the gesture but obliged and shook with his good arm. "Ruth, huh? That was my great-grandmother's name."

"You'd be surprised how often I hear that," she said, ending with an embarrassed chuckle.

Thomas merely snorted indignantly in reply.

The elevator chimed, indicating that they had reached the sixth floor. They stood in an awkward silence as they waited for the doors to open. She was two steps out of the elevator when Thomas decided to speak again.

"I look forward to your reports." That was all he said, and Dr. Waters had no time to respond before the doors closed and he was gone. But truth be told, she was glad to be rid of him. She turned away from the elevator and began making her way down the hall toward the Hayeses' room.

The elevator doors opened again on the tenth floor, and Thomas walked down the long hallway toward his new office. *His* office. It still had an exciting feeling to it. It made him prideful despite the unfortunate events that led to his promotion.

Multiple Lab workers acknowledged him as he passed, saying "Good morning, Director" in small voices Thomas appreciated the wariness with which they addressed him. In his previous position, he was a mere worker bee, given only the most basic respect. But now? He was a man to be feared. He liked that. He liked that *very much.*

He entered his office and walked over to the desk. Behind the big wooden piece of furniture was a floor-to-ceiling window that stretched across the entire wall. From here he could see the big field littered with trees, the same view Jade had from her tiny window.

His face twisted at the thought of her. He didn't understand why Dr. Peters had wanted to make her living quarters more comfortable. Why did it matter? What mattered was that they had gotten her. That *he* had gotten her. And as far as Thomas was concerned, she was nothing but another lab rat. There was nothing in the world that could convince him that she was anything but that.

After all, she did kill James, a small voice said, creeping up from the deep corners of his mind. The thought of Officer White immediately made his throat tighten. The image of his dear friend of twenty long years lying dead in the grass popped into his head and got stuck there. He couldn't unsee the hole that had been punched through James's chest. *The hole Jade had put there when she made those fucking trucks explode.* And even after all of that, she had gotten away. She had *lived*, and was *still* alive, and there was nothing he could do about it. But knowing that the torture of the experiments was resuming made it a little easier.

V

Bennett began by retelling his first meeting with Jade. He talked about how he'd stumbled upon her, with her dirty clothes and broken foot, in the middle of the woods. He mentioned how scared she'd looked. Dr. Waters took notes throughout the story.

Lewis had just told her about the first time the two officers, whose names he couldn't quite remember, came to the house when she interrupted.

"So you both knowingly lied to law enforcement regarding the whereabouts of Jade Cooper?" She asked. There was no contempt in her voice, no accusing tone. She didn't even look up from what she was writing. Lewis and Bennett looked at each other for a short moment before both nodding.

"Yes."

"And what came over you both to do such a thing?" She looked up at them now. "I mean, you both seem like law-abiding citizens. Neither of you has any hint of a criminal record. So why now?"

They sat quietly, thinking.

"Well," Bennett began, shifting in his seat a little. Lewis placed a hand firmly on his husband's knee.

"Because of Jade. She needed help. She was alone." He paused, and Dr. Waters took the opportunity to interject.

"But you said yourself, within the first hour she spent at your house, she displayed her inhuman ability to you both. Wasn't it clear to you then that she didn't *need* the help of two random men?"

Bennett's brows furrowed and a frown appeared on his face as he looked at the woman in front of him.

"That's not what I meant. We knew that she didn't really need us *physically*. There's nothing we could have done that she couldn't have done on her own tenfold. But she was *alone* and *scared*. And she's just a kid, you know?" He went quiet again.

Dr. Waters made more notes, and, on the inside, she was cheering. She knew that they cared about Jade, but hearing it for herself made what she was doing that much more important, and the plan more solidified.

She finished what she was writing and flipped through the other pages. She took out two pages that were stapled together, along with four or five sheets of blank paper. She set them down on the table and silently slid them across to Lewis and Bennett. She took a pen from one of her coat pockets and placed it on top of the paper so it didn't make a noise against the table. She stood, with a smile on her face.

"I suppose we will stop here for today. It was lovely seeing you gentlemen, and I will see you again this time tomorrow." With that, she went to the door, gave a small knock, and waited for one of the guards outside to let her out.

When she was gone, Lewis and Bennett sat in silence for a while until they were sure (*or as sure as they could be*) that no one was on the other side of the door. They looked at each other, and then down at the sheets of paper on the table. With a slightly shaking hand, Bennett removed the pen and picked up the stapled pages, holding them out in front of him so that they could both see what was written.

> *DO NOT READ ALOUD OR TALK ALOUD ABOUT ANYTHING THAT IS WRITTEN ON THE NEXT PAGE!! THIS IS A MATTER OF LIFE AND DEATH.*

They stared, stupefied, at the words scrawled across the paper. Bennett turned the page, and they began reading their escape plan.

VI

Do you trust her?

I don't know. But I know our options for people to trust are really limited right now.

Do you think she really means it? That she's planning on getting us and Jade out of here?

I hope so.

I just don't understand why. What does she have to gain by going against the very facility that she works for? There's no way she isn't risking EVERYTHING by doing this.

A noise in the hall made both Lewis's and Bennett's heads shoot up from their hunched positions over the piece of paper on the table. They sat silently, barely breathing, as they listened for any indication that someone was about to enter the room. They heard nothing. They bent over the page again and Bennett wrote his response.

Yeah, I'm confused about it too. But what else do we have?

Lewis dragged a hand down his face and sighed. Bennett wrapped an arm around Lewis's waist and squeezed.

"We'll be ok," Bennett whispered. Lewis nodded and laid his head on Bennett's shoulder.

Jade barely slept for the next two days. Her head was plagued by migraines, as it always was after a new dose of TK9. Multiple times each day, Lab workers would come in to do various tests on her—taking her vitals, checking her brain activity. They constantly had to have her connected to an IV because she was barely able to keep any kind of food or water down. Yet another perk of the TK9 serum.

But by the third day, the migraines had faded into dull headaches, and she was able to eat and sleep. And according to ritual, very early on the fourth day Jade was escorted to the giant gymnasium-like room where she would have to use her abilities so that the Lab could see if anything had changed.

Dr. Waters was there, surrounded by various other Lab workers and guards. The woman tried giving Jade a welcoming smile, which Jade did not return. She was too exhausted to do anything other than what they required of her. And she might not even be able to do that.

Situated around the very large room were weights of many different sizes and other—more specific—objects. The weights ranged from five pounds to three hundred tons. The objects included a baseball, a refrigerator, and one of the heavily armored trucks, like the ones they used to transport Jade and the other children the day she escaped.

As two of the Lab workers were hooking up the EEG and EKG machines to Jade, Dr. Waters approached.

"Good morning, Jade," the doctor began. "I know that you are very familiar with all of this, but because I am new to your process, I'm going to quickly go over the basics with you." Jade looked at her blankly, too tired to really care what the woman was saying. She gave a small nod.

"Today, we are to begin with your testing after your newest dose of the TK9 serum. We will begin by having you lift or move our smaller objects to allow your body to 'warm up.' Like stretching before doing an exercise." She glanced down at her clipboard and then back at Jade. "After you have worked your way up to the ten-pound mark, we will begin adding weight, going up by ten- to fifty-pound intervals."

Jade nodded again. The two Lab workers finally finished with their setup and retreated over to where their machinery was set up.

"All right, let's begin then." Dr. Waters turned so that she was looking in the direction of the first few objects. She backed up a couple of steps so that she was just behind Jade. "If you'd please start with Object 1: the baseball, please."

A moment after the words left her mouth, the air in the room gained a slight buzzing feeling. It never ceased to send chills down spines. Everyone watched the baseball intently. The Lab workers looked hurriedly back and forth from the machines receiving data to the ball. Dr. Waters was only looking at Jade.

The girl did not move. She didn't even shift her weight from one foot to the other. Yet the ball began to move. It rocked back and forth three times before a small shadow formed beneath it and it was floating. But then, the five-pound weight beside it also started to rise. And then the ten, the twenty, the thirty. All the objects and weight leading up to—and including—roughly one thousand pounds was hovering four feet in the air in a matter of seconds. And Jade wasn't breaking a sweat. To Dr. Waters, she almost seemed bored. Like she was close to falling asleep.

It really was lightweight for Jade. But it was the ease with which she was able to lift all these things that created a sort of excited yet anxious feeling in her stomach. She was a little scared of how much more she could do with just the single new dose of TK9. But oh, how she wanted to find out. And soon. She dropped everything, causing a loud *bang*, not unlike a gunshot, to echo through the gymnasium. The tile flooring under the heavier weights dented or cracked. When the sound cleared, Jade turned her head slightly to look over her shoulder expectantly at Dr. Waters.

"Right," the woman said in a small voice. Her ears (along with everyone else's) were ringing slightly. "Lets—" She was cut off by a very loud scraping sound. Everyone's heads turned toward the noise. At the far end of the gym, the three-hundred-ton weight was dragging across the tile, leaving behind deep gouges in the flooring. It picked up speed. It was only when it started really going fast that Dr. Waters and everyone else simultaneously realized that it was moving straight toward them.

In a blink it was off the ground and flying, at an even greater speed. Everyone dropped down to the ground as it flew overhead, missing a few of them by mere inches, and crashed through the wall. The whole room shook. The guards in the room immediately started drawing their guns and trying to aim them at Jade through the cloud of dust created by the destroyed wall.

"Don't shoot!" Dr. Waters shouted, knowing, without having to see any of them, what was happening. "Do not shoot!" She staggered to get to her feet, groping her coat pocket as she did so. Her heart stopped when she realized she couldn't feel the remote that she *knew* had been there. The remote that would administer the serums in Jade's collar was gone. Dr. Waters turned, slowly, to face Jade where she still stood, seemingly unfazed. Dr. Waters hadn't noticed that one of Jade's hands had been hidden behind her back until it slowly started to come forward. There in her hand, Jade held the remote. Dr. Waters's eyes widened, her heart pounding in her chest.

No, she thought. *Damn it! She's going to ruin everything!*

But Jade didn't press the button that would have released the collar from around her neck, although she knew exactly what to push. Instead, without ever breaking eye contact with the woman trembling before her, she extended her arm and held the remote out for Dr. Waters to take.

Slowly, the woman moved, took a step toward Jade. But the moment her fingers closed around the remote, she found herself incapable of moving. A chill ran through her body. Her skin felt like it was buzzing. And as suddenly as it had started, it stopped. The message Jade was sending her—"Do not fuck with me"—was very clear, and by god, Dr. Waters was going to respect it.

Jade was escorted back to her room by the guards, leaving Dr. Waters and the other Lab workers behind in the ruined room. The doctor stared at the doors Jade had disappeared through for a long time. A small smile worked its way onto her face.

From his office, Thomas watched in horror as the entire encounter in the gymnasium took place on the screen of his computer.

"Don't you ever worry?" Thomas asked the man sitting opposite him in his office. "Don't you worry that you're giving her *too much*?" He leaned forward against his desk. "I mean, what living thing deserves that much *power*?"

The other man sighed and folded his hands in his lap. Dr. Peters had arrived early that morning. He'd come to Thomas first thing, wanting a report on how everyone—especially Jade—was adjusting after the capture. He leaned back in his chair and sighed once more as he looked at Thomas.

"There's something you need to know, which I could not have told you over the phone. And there really is no way that I can ease you into it, so I'll just say it. Jade Cooper is the only living subject of our experimentation."

There was silence. Thomas was dumbfounded. He leaned back in his own chair slowly, his eyes never leaving Dr. Peters.

"What?" he finally said, not quite able to comprehend it.

Dr. Peters hesitated before getting out of his seat and slowly walking around the desk to stand in front of the giant windows.

"I know neither you nor your former partner was informed of the purpose for the transportation of those four subjects." He paused, staring out the window. "They were being taken to our much smaller sister facility across the country. There, our fellow scientists were to take as many blood samples as possible from each subject for further testing. We couldn't do it here because we simply had too many other projects that required our attention.

"The goal was to keep all of our most powerful products contained in the same highly guarded location. It was becoming too dangerous to keep them here, with the others. And besides, Jade had developed a second ability. Do you realize how *rare* that is? Of the hundreds of subjects that we have tested on, *she is the only one*. We needed as many available minds as we could spare to see what it was about her that allowed such a thing to happen.

"And because of that, when we got word here about the incident that led to one of our subjects' escape, there was a mass panic in our facility. My other colleagues and I rashly made the decision to eliminate any chance that such a thing might ever happen again. So we put the order out for all the other subjects in the facility to be terminated." He paused for a moment. "After the two massacres, the goal of your team was to eliminate her as well. But then we all got to thinking logically, and we decided that it would be easier to attempt to capture Jade and bring her back here than it was to completely start over. So at the last minute the objective was changed. Luckily, it worked. Unfortunately, there were casualties, but that was to be expected."

A spark of rage flickered in Thomas's stomach. He was angry with Dr. Peters for keeping something as important as this from him. And he was also frustrated with himself for not even *noticing* that there were no other subjects around. *How could he have missed that?* He stayed silent.

Dr. Peters turned now to look at Thomas. He could see the anger in the director's eyes, but he paid it no mind.

"Everything that this organization is, and ever will be, now lies on Jade's shoulders," Dr. Peters added. Thomas thought for a moment.

"And Michael?" he asked. He didn't know why his mind went to the small boy who could turn into a monster, but it did. Dr. Peters nodded.

"Ah, yes. Michael. Michael was initially supposed to be used to capture and kill Jade. After that, the team had been instructed to kill him as well. It would have been easy, too, because of the mind controlling serum." He shook his head. "But, as it turned out, he was bound to die either way."

Thomas didn't know why the doctor's response made him even angrier, but it did. He practically had steam coming out of his ears. He never felt so much like a pawn in his whole life. Not even when he was just a cop. And now his pride was hurt. That's what really ignited the flame.

VII

Jade studied herself in the bathroom mirror. She stared at the dark bags that had formed under her eyes, at the metal collar that was secured firmly around her throat.

A part of her truly had wanted to press the button on Dr. Waters's remote that would have allowed her to remove it. She had wanted to try her hand at another escape. But then she had thought about the power that she had just displayed, and how she might be able to get more of that. And she thought about Lewis and Bennett. About the fact that they might be somewhere in this building with her, and that she was going to need all that the Lab could give her to get all three of them out of here. If she'd tried today, she may have failed. She might have gotten them killed.

Her eyes watered a little at the thought of them. They were here, in this nightmare of a place, because of her. Because they had helped her. She felt extremely guilty about it. She watched a tear slip down her face and wiped it away tiredly. She was going to get them out of here, she decided. She would endure the torture for them.

Another tear fell, slipping all the way down her cheek and neck until it hit the collar. She stared at the ugly metal thing for a long time before a light flickered in her brain. She leaned over the sink to look at it more carefully. After searching for some time, she found what she was looking for.

There were dozens of tiny screws that held the two main halves of the collar together. Her heart was beating fast as her mind played with the idea. She took a deep breath and braced herself. She concentrated on one of the screws and watched as it slowly started turning. It turned and turned and turned until suddenly falling with a clink into the sink. Jade scrambled to catch it with her hands before it had time to roll down the drain.

She froze. She was waiting for any kind of indication that the collar was about to explode, or administer the serums locked inside. She had no idea what—if anything at all—might happen after any kind of tampering with the collar. But after a few moments of shallow breathing and silence, there was nothing. She sighed deeply and squeezed her eyes shut momentarily. When she opened them again, she was met with her own reflection. There was a new light in her eyes that was nowhere to be found just minutes before. She looked at the collar again.

In a matter of two agonizingly slow minutes, Jade held twenty-five tiny screws in her left hand and both halves of the metal collar in her right. She stared at the device in her hands with scared wonder. She carefully set the screws onto the flat surface of the back of the toilet. She rotated both halves of the collar in her hands, studying them. She turned them over so that she was looking inside, at the innermost part that touched her throat.

She could clearly see the vials of the mind controlling serum. Her stomach turned at the sight of the murky red substance. With her fingers, she very carefully tried to pry the vials out of their compartments. They came out much more easily than she thought they would, and soon she had all six lined up next to the screws. They were small, no bigger than her thumb. But they packed one hell of a punch. She shuddered as she remembered the darts filled with the same liquid—how she had lost control of her body and how everything had gone black. They could have made her do *anything*.

Anger started to build in her stomach. Her chest felt like it was filled with stones. She quickly knocked the vials into the toilet bowl and flushed. She watched them as they spiraled down and disappeared. The anger was still there, but a little bit of the heaviness in her chest lessened once they were gone. She then carefully placed the two halves of the collar around her throat again and held them there as one by one the small screws moved from the back of the toilet and screwed themselves back into place.

One more, she thought as she looked at herself once more in the bathroom mirror. *I'll allow them to do one more dose of the TK9 serum. And then I'm getting us out of here.*

She left the bathroom and began thinking of a plan to get Lewis, Bennett, and herself away from the Lab. She sat on the edge of her bed, looking up at the window as she thought.

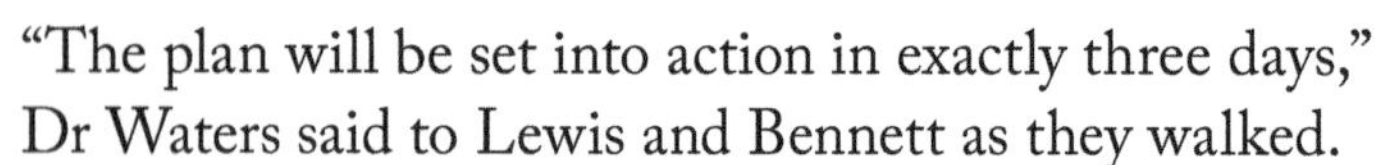

"The plan will be set into action in exactly three days," Dr Waters said to Lewis and Bennett as they walked.

She had managed to convince Dr. Peters and Director O'Riley to allow the Hayeses some time outdoors. "It does them no good to be locked up in the building the whole time. And we need them to tell us all the information that they gained in their time with Jade. We won't get that if they grow restless and unhappy," she'd said to them. She had been required to wear a wire during the entire walk around the building. But before she'd gone to get Lewis and Bennett this morning, the microphone had broken. Nothing that was to be said would be recorded. What a shame.

"Three days?" Bennett asked in a low voice. Behind the trio were two guards. They were following about forty feet behind, but they still needed to be careful. It was made extremely clear that no one should hear about what they were doing. "That feels like a long time," he added.

Dr. Waters sighed and nodded her head. "I know, but unfortunately, it's the best I can do. There are two procedures scheduled for Jade over the next two days, and Dr. Peters will be watching her like a hawk. Only the day after her second procedure will he even allow anyone other than himself to oversee any tests."

Lewis's next step forward faltered a little, but he caught himself quickly. "Procedures?" he asked in a strained voice. He hated the sound of that. They both did.

Dr. Waters continued to look straight ahead. "Yes, procedures," she said simply.

Bennett scoffed and raised his eyebrows at her lame response. "Care to elaborate a little?"

She looked at them then, but only for a moment. She could see anger and concern in Bennett's face, worry and fear in Lewis's. She looked away.

"The experimentation on Jade Cooper resumed three days after you were all taken into custody." She did not tell them about the scene Jade had made in the gymnasium. She didn't think it was safe for them to know.

Lewis's face visibly paled, and Bennett looked down at the ground under his feet. *Experimentation* kept echoing in both of their brains. They couldn't help but imagine the pain she was in, both physically and mentally. To have almost been free of this place, and these people, only to be dragged right back again. Repeating the same old patterns. It must be traumatizing.

They wondered whether she thought about them. If she ever wondered—or worried—about where they ended up after they were taken. But neither of them would ever blame her if she didn't. She had too much else going on to worry about two people she barely knew.

"What does Jade say about all this?" Lewis asked. "About your plan?"

Dr. Waters was silent for a moment. "Jade doesn't know about my plan," she said finally. "And she can't ever know. Not until it's already in action."

Lewis and Bennett frowned. They looked at each other briefly in confusion, and then back to Dr. Waters.

"What?" Bennett asked.

"Why not?" Lewis added.

"Because it would be too dangerous if she knew anything. There's a specialized device that the Lab has made into collars for the subjects that contains mind controlling serums. I'm sure you remember the one that the boy Michael was wearing that day at your cabin. It has been made very clear that Jade is to always wear one of these collars. If any of my colleagues were to become suspicious, they could easily force Jade to tell them everything she knows."

"Why are you doing this?" Bennett suddenly blurted out before he could seriously consider the consequences of his question. "I mean—what do you possibly have to gain? You don't know us. We don't even know if you knew Jade before all this. And you're obviously involved in all the stuff that's happening here. So—" he hesitated; swallowed hard. Lewis grabbed his hand and squeezed. "*Why?*" Bennett finally finished.

It caught Dr. Waters completely off guard, and she immediately stopped walking. She stood silently, starting at the two men who stared back at her expectantly. She knew they must have been curious, must have had doubts. But she never really thought that it would be so important to them that they bothered to ask. But here they were. And they were waiting.

She looked away from them, back in the direction they had been walking, her eyes darting back and forth across the horizon as she thought. Then she started walking again, slowly, and they followed.

"I had a little girl, once," she announced in a barely audible voice. Her eyes started to sting. She cleared her throat to get rid of some of the tightness that was building. "I had a little girl, and she got sick," she continued. "I took her to every hospital that every specialist ever recommended, but nothing changed. No one could figure out what was wrong with her." She fought the tears that were building in her eyes. "I got desperate. And I knew that I worked with some of the greatest minds in scientific history. So I contacted Dr. Peters and asked him for help.

"I knew what kind of research he did because I was very involved with the experimentation process. He said that he would put together a special team to try to create something that would cure my daughter. And that's exactly what he did. After rigorous testing and multiple reroutes, they finally came up with something that they thought might work. And it did." She paused. A tear slipped down her face, and she made no move to wipe it away.

"She started to get better, and I was so relieved. I was so grateful for the second chance that they were giving me with my daughter.

"But they got greedy." Her face darkened and her brows furrowed. She glared out into the distance. "They started adjusting the serums that they were giving her. They told me that the new additions would keep her from getting sick again, that they were trying to cure her permanently.

"But they were actually giving her new serums that they had been developing for the subjects. They had begun experimenting on her for their own research. And by the time I realized what was happening—" Her voice caught in her throat. More tears slipped. Beside her, Lewis and Bennett were also letting tears fall.

"My daughter was killed by those serums," she finally managed to say. Her chest was growing tight, and it was becoming more and more difficult to breathe. "When I had confronted Dr. Peters about everything that had been going on, he acted as if he had no idea that any of it was happening. But I knew better. There isn't a single experiment that takes place without his signature of approval." She cleared her throat again.

Bennett wiped his face with the heel of his palm.

Lewis stared down at the ground. His grip on Bennett's hand had grown exponentially tighter since the beginning of Dr. Waters's story.

The doctor sighed deeply, trying to release some of the tension that had built up in her body, but it didn't really work.

"Since then, I have been waiting. Keeping myself under the radar. Not working with anything regarding experimentation." She glanced over at Lewis and Bennett briefly.

"Over a decade I've been waiting. Waiting for something—anything—that I could really use to take this fucking place down.

"Then the incident that led to Jade's escape took place. And then Dr. Peters and the other uppers panicked and had all the other subjects killed. Now, Jade is all they have left."

She did not look at Lewis and Bennett again for the remainder of the walk.

"So to answer your question simply, I'm doing this for my little girl. For Jade, who never got to be one. And for you, because I know you'll take care of her."

VIII

Thomas wanted to see it all as it happened in person instead of watching it on a screen from the safety of his office. He'd been feeling restless lately from sitting behind a desk instead of doing any physical work. He knew he wasn't really cut out for a filling-out-papers or giving-out-orders-while-he-just-sat-back-and-watched kind of gig. But the power that came with the job blinded him. And he figured that if he could at least go down to the labs and watch the subject squirm a little, it would be good enough for now. He was also still very unnerved about the meeting he'd had with Dr. Peters.

He stood on the other side of the two-way mirror among many Lab workers who scurried around, checking their machines. He'd just watched them hook up the EEG and EKG to Jade. She looked small, sitting in that big white chair.

She was sitting there, blank faced, waiting for one of the Lab workers to come in and give her the new dose. It made Thomas a little annoyed. He wanted to see fear, or anger, or sadness in her face. Or at the very least a little *distress.* But she just looked tired. Like she could fall asleep at any minute, there in that chair.

And she *was* tired. Jade had been up all night plotting. She only managed to fall asleep an hour before they came to get her. She really might have fallen asleep then. But the door to the big white room opened, and her heart started racing.

The EKG started spitting out paper with her rapid heart rate printed in black ink. Thomas didn't bother fighting the smile that stretched across his face. *There it is*, he thought. *There's the fear.*

Dr. Peters was the cause of that fear. When Dr. Peters was in the room, Jade knew that things were going to hurt, that the tests were going to be more extreme than a simple poke with a needle.

"Hello, Jade," he said. The very sound of his voice made her skin break out into goose flesh. He stepped aside—allowing a Lab worker to wheel in a cart—and grabbed a chair from beside the door. He dragged it over so that he was sitting right in front of her as the Lab worker was adjusting the objects on the cart. Jade saw some of them gleaming in the fluorescent lights from the corner of her eye. She didn't dare turn her head to look.

"You've had yourself quite the adventure since the last time I saw you," he continued. The Lab worker finished what he was doing and hurriedly left the room. Jade was breathing heavily through her nose as she stared at the man before her. Her eyes shifted back and forth, up and down, across his face and body. She didn't know what she was looking for exactly, but she didn't want to be surprised by anything he might do. A small smile formed on his face.

"I'm glad you're back," he said, and reached over toward the cart. Jade flinched as his hand came near her. She instinctively tried scooting back in the chair as far as she could as his hand came back to him, carrying a syringe. She stared at it and her face paled. The liquid inside wasn't the regular milky-white color of the TK9. This was a grayish pink color. It was the serum that gave Jade her self-healing ability. A knot formed in her stomach.

"You know, you were always my favorite." He looked down briefly at the syringe. He was rolling it between his fingers. The lights above made the liquid inside look like it was glowing. He shrugged his shoulders and looked back up at her. "And it would have been really unfortunate to have to start all over with all of this." He gestured widely and Jade winced. Her eyes were moving back and forth between his face and his hands. He stood so that he was looking down at her. Jade's heart was hammering in her chest.

"Besides," he continued. "You're the only one we've ever had that developed more than one ability with our serums. And something like that is too precious to lose." He finished with a slight frown. Before Jade could react, the needle was in her throat and he was pushing the plunger. She gritted her teeth as the needle left her skin.

Instantly the burning sensation began as the serum spread through her body. She couldn't help but squirm around in the chair. Her jaw stayed locked as she tried to hold back the scream of pain that was trying to crawl its way up and out of her throat. The muscles in her shoulder and neck seized, and if she hadn't been wearing the collar, she would have slammed her head into her shoulder. She squeezed her eyes shut and was holding her breath trying to stay silent. Dr. Peters frowned.

"Does it hurt?" he asked, resting his hands on his knees so that he was at her level. A small sound escaped her that cascaded into a full shriek of pain. The lights above them flickered for a moment. The air had that buzzing feeling to it. Dr. Peters stood up straight again, shaking his head.

"Now, now, Jade. You'd better get yourself under control." He turned toward the cart and grabbed a pair of latex gloves. Jade opened her eyes just enough to see him. The burning was in her fingertips, in her chest. She could feel it migrating down her legs toward her feet. Her scalp was prickly with the feeling. It was becoming slightly more bearable. Dr. Peters picked up one of the three tools that were laid out on the cart.

"Well, now, the serum should be just about everywhere in your body at this point." He examined the blade in his hand as he spoke. "Unfortunately, that means we need to move on to the testing phase, I'm afraid." He looked down at her. She saw nothing in his eyes. She couldn't pick out a single emotion. And it made the entire encounter scarier. An empty vessel has no regard for the people he is affecting. At least if there'd been something behind those eyes, she would have hoped that somewhere deep inside, he felt a little bad about the things he did. But there was nothing.

With a quick movement, he grabbed the top of her head firmly with his free hand and pushed it against the headrest of the chair. Jade grimaced as the cool blade of the scalpel cut through the flesh of her cheek one, two, three, four times straight across. Dr. Peters shifted to the other side and cut four more gashes in her other cheek. She could immediately feel the blood beginning to roll down her face and pool around the collar. Dr. Peters placed the scalpel back onto the cart, changed his gloves, and grabbed a tool that looked very much like a thin, metal nutcracker.

Quickly, he grabbed hold of her first and middle fingers on her right hand, placed them between the metal clamps, and with a swift and powerful squeeze, broke her fingers. Jade screamed, and the tool in his hand flew across the room. Without missing a beat, Dr. Peters smacked her across the face. On impact, blood sprayed, leaving little red dots on her clothes, the chair, the floor, and the sleeve of his coat. Her face and his gloved hand were smeared red. He firmly grabbed hold of her face with his stained hand. His fingers dug into the cuts on her cheeks. Tears were streaming down her face, but she didn't dare make a sound.

"Now, I told you to control yourself," he said in a low voice, then he roughly let go of her face. Blood started to flow more heavily from her cheeks. Her tears left pink streaks.

He started shaking his head a little as he looked at her. Like he was disappointed. He huffed and walked across the room to where the tool had landed and picked it up. He brought it back over to the chair where Jade sat. He stood motionless for a moment, holding the metal clamp in both of his hands. He was looking at her, but it didn't look like he was really seeing her. It was like he was looking through her. Like he was thinking. His eyes suddenly shifted a little.

"You know the consequence," he said, but he didn't move. "I was going to leave your other hand alone, since it's been a while since we've seen each other. But I can't do that now." With that, he grabbed hold of her left hand. She couldn't help but fight back a little, trying to pull her hand away despite the restraints around her wrists. His elbow struck the side of her face. Her eyes suddenly went out of focus, and a ringing started in her ear. He took advantage of her disorientation, grabbed her hand firmly, stuck the last three fingers on her left hand between the clamps, and squeezed. She could hear the bones snapping above the ringing in her ear, and she started screaming again. She was sobbing, tears pouring down her face. But no tools went flying across the room this time.

The blood on her cheeks was being washed away by her tears as it poured out of her wounds. The fingers on her right hand were already starting to turn purple. They had already swollen to double their original size. She could feel her rapid heartbeat in her hands. Without a word, Dr. Peters turned and left the room.

For a long moment, Thomas watched Jade as she sat alone in the big white room, screaming between sobs, before he too left without saying a word.

IX

Jade stared at herself in the bathroom mirror. Her whole body was trembling, and she looked like she'd been attacked by an animal. The gouges in her cheeks were deeper than she'd thought they were. Her face and neck were still covered in drying blood. The Lab workers hadn't bothered to clean her up before sending her back to her room. Her eyes were puffy and red from crying. Her purple, swollen hands were held up in front of her chest. She couldn't stop her face from twisting into a painful grimace as she continued to look at herself.

Her eyes started to sting, and a lump formed in her throat. She swallowed hard and tried taking deep breaths. But a rogue tear slipped, and the composure ended there. Her knees went wobbly, and she took a few sloppy steps backward until her back hit the wall behind her and she sank down to the floor. She hugged her injured hands to her chest as she sobbed. Her salty tears made the cuts on her cheeks sting. Her head was throbbing. She let out a scream. It was a frustrated, pain-filled scream that caused the whole building to shake. The glass mirror on the wall splintered.

Lewis and Bennett felt the rumble beneath their feet in their room two floors above Jade's. Some of the lighter furniture in their room, like the chairs, started sliding across the floor due to the vibration. Neither of them moved from the bed where they sat until the rumbling stopped. They looked at each other, bewildered, eyes wide and mouths slightly agape like they each wanted to say something. Somehow, both knew instantly that it had something to do with Jade. Whether she was the one who did it or not, they couldn't know.

They waited anxiously for Dr. Waters to come to their room for their daily morning meeting. They hoped she'd have some kind of answer for them.

Dr. Waters steadied herself against a wall as she waited for the earthquake-like trembling of the floor to stop. A knot formed in her stomach. This morning was scheduled to be Jade's first meeting with Dr. Peters since her arrival back at the Lab. Dr. Waters knew that the other doctor's personal methods were much harsher than any of the other Lab workers'. She just hoped he hadn't gone too far. That none of it would prevent her from going forward with her plan.

She hurried down the hall toward Lewis and Bennett's room. As she reached the door, she paused for a moment. She closed her eyes, took a deep breath, and gave a small knock to the heavy metal door before opening it and entering the room.

Lewis and Bennett stood from the bed immediately as she entered. She quickly put a finger to her lips as she closed the door behind her and started for the table. They followed, not saying a word. She could feel the energy coming off of them. The three of them took their seats and she started fishing for a blank sheet of paper from her clipboard. She took a pen from her coat pocket and started writing.

"Good morning, gentlemen." She said her usual greeting. "How are you feeling this morning?" It took them a moment to respond.

"Fine," they answered in unison. Dr. Waters nodded as she finished what she was writing. She turned the paper around for them to read.

"Good, good." she answered aloud. "Are you ready to begin?"

They both nodded absentmindedly as they stared down at the paper on the table.

That was her, the paper read. *I don't know what happened, but we need to be extremely careful.*

Three hours had passed since Jade had been returned to her room, and she was still sitting on the bathroom floor. She was exhausted. Her head throbbed, and she could still faintly feel her pulse in her broken fingers. She stared up at the broken mirror, its shards still somehow intact. She couldn't help the humorless smile that spread across her face. The blood caked on her cheeks and neck cracked and flaked off with the stretching of skin. Her face twisted in sudden pain for a quick moment before the smile faltered and she was blank-faced.

She had smiled because she very much felt like that mirror right now. A bunch of broken pieces somehow still stuck together.

It's ok if you're not ok, She heard Lewis's voice say from somewhere in her mind. *You're allowed to not be ok all the time.*

The memory made her want to cry again. She really missed them. She'd give anything to see Lewis and Bennett again. Just one more time. To hear their voices. She wanted to hug them, and she'd never wanted a hug from anyone so much in her whole life. They made her feel *safe.* And they had made her feel…loved? Was that what love felt like? Jade knew hate like an old friend. But love was foreign. She sighed and closed her eyes. She started thinking about the memories she had between the time Bennett found her and when they were taken. She knew she loved them. And whether they loved her or not didn't really matter, she decided. She was going to help them, just like they had helped her.

She struggled to her feet and hesitated a moment before looking at her jagged reflection in the mirror.

I guess it's time for another test, she thought with a sigh. She took a deep breath and let it out slowly, concentrating on her face intently. She could feel the burning of the new serum start and stop suddenly as she began to use her self-healing ability. It started up again and slowly moved from her chest up her neck and into her face. A faint, glowing white light started to emanate from deep within the gashes in her cheeks. It stung, but she kept pushing until she could see the wounds starting to close. She watched as the split skin started to fuse back together, and after a long minute, there was no evidence that anything had happened to her face. Well, except for all the blood. But there weren't any scars, or anything else, that would hint at a previous injury. She became slightly lightheaded, but only for a moment.

She looked down at her hands and groaned. This was about to be hell and she knew it. It was going to be worse than when she'd healed her broken foot, that was for sure. This might even be worse than when Dr. Peters broke them. A chill ran down her spine at the mere thought of the man.

She gave a quick glance around the room. She needed to find something to bite into while she did this. But there was nothing in the bathroom that she could use. She turned toward the door and, very carefully, used her wrists to turn the doorknob and push open the door.

She looked around the room for a few moments before finally deciding that the blanket on her bed was going to be her best option. She gingerly stuffed one corner of the fabric in her teeth and sat down on the edge of the mattress. She took a deep breath in and out through her nose and started concentrating on her right hand. She stared intently at the first and middle fingers that were royally swollen and purple. A blue-green and yellow bruise stretched in a circle almost past her thumb around her whole hand.

The burning started again in her chest and began moving down her arm, into her hand, and into her fingertips. Immediately, she could feel the muscles and the bones starting to shift under her skin and her whole hand felt like it was on fire. She bit down hard on the fabric between her teeth and let out a muffled yell. She could hear sickening popping sounds as her bones quickly fused back together. She started to feel a little lightheaded, and she couldn't tell if it was because of the pain or the healing. She continued anyway. She watched as the bruise started to fade some. The swelling started going down rapidly. She stopped healing herself with a heavy sigh, spitting the blanket out of her mouth. She hesitated, and then tried bending the fingers on her right hand. No pain. She sighed, relieved, but groaned as she remembered the other hand.

She had just finished healing her left hand, which had been much worse than her right, when there was a knock at the door.

PART THREE

Petrichor

(n.) the smell of earth after rain

I

Jade stood in the middle of the room, staring at the door. She knew she was going to be one hell of a sight to whoever walked in. Dried blood still covered her lower face and neck. Dr. Peters entered the room. When he saw her, a grin formed on his face.

"Ah, I see you've already gotten yourself fixed up," he marveled. He looked at her up and down with one quick movement of his eyes as he moved across the room. He stopped about six feet in front of her. His grin widened, and he held his hands behind his back. "Seems to me like the alterations to that serum paid off, no?"

Jade glared at him from where she stood. Rage was building inside of her with every second that passed. Seeing him standing there, *smiling*, like he hadn't just tortured her four hours before—not to mention for the past ten years—made her furious. Her hands were starting to shake, and her jaw was clenching and unclenching as she tried to focus. His arms suddenly came forward, hands clasping in front of him, and the sudden movement made her flinch. He frowned, but Jade could tell it wasn't sincere.

"Oh, don't be like that," he said, letting his arms drop so they were hanging at his sides. "I'm just here to see how you're doing, that's all. We aren't doing any more testing today."

"No," she said suddenly. "We're not." She was so filled with anger that she was sure her voice was going to come out shaky but was surprised—yet very thankful—by how steady and harsh her voice was. Dr. Peters was caught off guard that she even spoke at all, let alone so aggressively, and it showed clearly on his face. He stared at her, awestruck, for a few moments before a short, incredulous laugh burst from his lips.

"Excuse me?" he asked, taking a step toward her. She took a step back instinctively. "What did you say?"

"I said you're right. That we're not doing any more testing today."

His eyebrows rose, and his hands snaked their way into his coat pockets. He was shocked, still, by her boldness. His mouth opened, about to say something, then stopped. Confusion and a hint of fear filled his eyes as he suddenly realized that he was no longer able to breathe. A pressure had built around his throat and was gradually getting tighter by the second.

"And we won't be doing any more testing ever again."

His hands scrambled in his coat pockets before finally gaining a firm hold on the remote and pressing the button. Jade could feel the needles puncturing her throat, but nothing else. She took a step toward Dr. Peters, who promptly stepped backward. Panic was steadily taking hold of him, and his hands flew up to his throat, sending the remote sliding across the room. The pressure around his throat lessened some, and he quickly took in a shallow, wheezing breath.

He watched, eyes wide, as the collar around Jade's throat abruptly broke apart and fell to the ground at her feet. He tried making a break for the door but found that he could not move. Jade looked at him for a long time. She watched him struggling to breathe, wanting to escape but not being able to. And she finally thought that he was feeling just a tiny fraction of the things he had made her feel over the years. A small smile appeared on her face.

In a blink, his head whipped around to an unnatural angle, and she let his body crumble to the floor. Jade didn't bother taking a moment to look at his body, to revel in the fact that she had finally beaten him. Instead, with a quick flex of her fist, the door to the room exploded off its hinges. The huge, thick piece of metal flew inward and through the wall that held her tiny window. In four long strides, she was out in the hallway.

Immediately, she was met by five guards. They were still recovering from the shock of watching the door disappear and didn't have time to realize that she was about to walk past them. Not that it would have made a difference anyway. As she walked by, each of their necks snapped and they fell dead to the floor.

A knot had formed in Dr. Waters's stomach. Anxiety was starting to build in her chest for no apparent reason, and she knew something was wrong. She could almost feel it in the air.

The hairs on her arms stood on end as the white lights in the hall suddenly started blinking. She stood still, watching the light above her flicker. Her heartbeat was suddenly so loud that it was all she could hear.

"All authorized personnel report to floor four! This is a code nine emergency! I repeat, a code nine emergency!"

The voice blared over the speakers throughout the building. Dr. Waters's heart skipped a beat, and she felt like she was going to faint.

That's Jade's floor, she thought, and in an instant, she started sprinting down the hall toward the elevator. She mashed the button for the sixth floor with her fingers and repeatedly pressed the "close" button. Her stomach felt like it rose all the way up to her throat as she elevator descended.

Bennett's hands were shaking as he watched Lewis pacing the floor, biting his nails. It had been almost eight minutes since the intercom had announced an emergency taking place on the fourth floor.

They had both been anxious since their meeting with Dr. Waters that morning, and this wasn't making it any easier to deal with. It made it a little harder knowing that they weren't going to see Dr. Waters again, since she never came twice in one day. They were going to have to wait this out until tomorrow, when they could ask her what was going on.

"Do you think she's ok?" Bennett finally said. Lewis glanced at his husband and continued to pace. He folded his arms over his chest and shook his head absentmindedly.

"I don't know," he sighed. "But something's telling me she isn't."

"Do you think she's the reason for the announcements? That she's the emergency?"

"Probably," Lewis mumbled. He hadn't wanted to admit it, but he'd been wondering the same. *Knew* the same. Bennett stood from the edge of the bed and walked over to Lewis, wrapping his arms around him. Lewis could feel that Bennett's whole body was shaking. They stood like that for a while until the door to their room burst open with a loud bang. Dr. Waters was standing there, panting from running.

"We need to go," she huffed. "Right now."

"It's Jade, isn't it?" Bennett asked. Lewis was still held firmly in his arms, and it took a moment for Lewis to pry himself away.

Dr. Waters nodded. "Yes. I'm sure of it. I don't know what she's done, but everyone is occupied with it which means *we need to go*," she said hurriedly. "We're not going to get a better opportunity than this."

Before either of them had truly decided, they were running down the empty hall behind her.

11

The elevators were now disconnected because of the emergency, so Dr. Waters led them down through the stairwells. They had gone down only one floor before they had been forced to hug the walls so that armored men could get by them on their way to the fourth floor. None of them paid the trio any mind. Either they didn't know who Lewis and Bennett were or they simply did not care. There were more pressing matters to deal with than a couple of escaped nobodies.

When the way cleared again, they continued their descent. As they neared the fourth floor, however, they stopped. Muffled gunfire echoed in the hall beyond the door. The voices of two—maybe three—men suddenly filled the air before cutting off abruptly. Then the gunfire started waning until there was only one. There was a loud bang, completely different from the sounds of the gun, and then there was silence. They all held their breath as they stood in the stairwell.

Slowly, Dr. Waters crept toward the door and peeked through the small window. Her breath caught in her throat, making almost a strangled sort of sound. Her head turned to look at the two men who were staring at her wide-eyed, half expecting her to start sprinting down the stairs. Her face had gone pale, and this made Lewis and Bennett even more anxious. But then her hand rose, reached for the door handle, and turned it. The small clicking sound was deafening in the dead silent stairwell. She looked at them one more time before pulling the door open and holding it there for them to enter the hall.

They hesitated, looking back and forth between each other and Dr. Waters. Was she really trying to get them to go through there? After all the *gunfire* and the *emergency* that was supposed to be taking place there? *And what the hell did she see down the hall?* Bennett finally stepped forward, reluctantly, and Lewis had no choice but to follow him.

"Oh," Bennett breathed as he stepped past the door frame. He suddenly felt very lightheaded, and if Lewis hadn't been standing so close to him, he might have fallen over.

"Oh," Lewis copied. Dr. Waters closed the door behind her as she entered the hall after them. The sound made them both jump.

Dead bodies littered the floor. They couldn't help but notice that a lot of the bodies lay belly-to-floor, with their blank faces pointed up at the ceiling. Others had their limbs in impossible positions. There were huge spots of blood on the walls, floor, and ceiling where the three of them assumed some of their heads had been smashed. Lewis vomited, and Bennett was having trouble *not* vomiting. Dr. Waters stood silently just behind them.

Then a figure dressed in white stood from its crouched position at the other end of the hall, and everyone froze. There was blood streaked on its face and shirt. They all stood silently, completely still, staring at each other, almost daring the other to move first.

"Jade?" Bennett called. He hadn't planned on saying anything. It was more of a compulsion than a decision. He took a small step forward and Lewis grabbed his arm firmly. Bennett didn't try to walk forward again.

At the other end of the hall, Jade began to cry. She couldn't really believe that they were standing there. That she was *seeing* them there. And a weight formed in her chest because she was embarrassed that they had to see any of what she'd just done. The tears were streaming steadily down her face.

She started walking forward, slowly at first. With each step she took, the bodies on the floor started to slide to either side of the hall, leaving a clear path down the middle.

"It's her," Lewis breathed.

Relief filled Lewis and Bennett, and they also started walking to meet her. And as they moved forward, the bodies on their end of the hall started diverging. Then very quickly the two started running, and Jade started running, until they crashed into each other in the middle of the long hallway. Lewis and Bennett held her tightly between them. Jade was crying even harder now. A few tears fell down Lewis's and Bennett's faces also.

"God, we were so worried about you," Lewis said with a sad sort of laugh. Jade looked up at them.

"*Me?*" she asked, confusion clear in her saddened eyes. "You were worried about *me?* I've been worried about you! I had no idea what had happened to you guys!" Her voice cracked and her eyes welled with more tears. "I was afraid that you guys were—" But she didn't finish her sentence. Bennett sighed and hugged her tighter.

Dr. Waters watched them from where she still stood near the stairwell door. A tightness had built in her chest and in her throat. She smiled a sad—but also happy—smile. She knew that she was never getting her daughter back, but she knew that she could settle for them to get theirs.

"Are you all right?" Lewis asked. His brows were pulled in, and his eyes were searching Jade's face. He and Bennett had both been concerned about the blood on her face and were equally confused to see that there was no kind of cut or scratch. And they really didn't believe that it could be anybody else's blood. Jade nodded.

"I'm ok." She stepped back from them absentmindedly and took her shirt tail in her hands and wiped her cheeks. The wetness from her crying helped get quite a bit of the blood off, but her face was still stained red. "I'm ok *now*," she clarified. She could see that her declaration hadn't swayed them. She wanted to sit down with them right then and there and tell them everything and hear about what had happened to them since getting taken. But she had things to do. She needed to stop being distracted.

"I'll tell you later," she said. "I promise." She glanced around them, eyes shifting over all the bodies, before she noticed Dr. Waters and her face paled.

Lewis and Bennett noticed the change immediately and turned their heads to see what she was seeing. They had almost forgotten that the doctor had been with them at all. They had been too caught up in the reunion.

"It's ok!" Lewis said quickly. "She's been helping us."

Jade's gaze shifted warily back and forth between Dr. Waters and the two men standing before her. Cautiously, Dr. Waters started making her way down the hall to where they were all standing.

"Jade," Dr. Waters greeted her in a low voice. She was a little frightened. She knew that if Jade wanted to, she could get all three of them out of the building and away from the Lab in less time than it would take her dead body to hit the floor. But here she was, still standing. Jade only gave her a short nod in return. Her gaze lingered on Dr. Waters for a long moment before returning to Lewis and Bennett. The doctor took note of how Jade's gaze softened as she looked at them.

"You need to get out of here," Jade said abruptly. Both Lewis and Bennett tried to protest.

"What about you?" Lewis asked.

"We're not leaving here without you," Bennett balked.

Jade nodded furiously. "Yes, you are," she said, and she looked at Dr. Waters. "And you're going to get them out."

"Of course," Dr. Waters replied immediately. "That was always the plan." Jade nodded, and Dr. Waters could see something change in her face.

"Jade, please," Bennett said. "You can't make us leave here without you. We just got you back! We can't lose you again!" Small smiles formed on both Jade's and Dr. Waters's faces. They both knew that yes, technically, she absolutely could *make* them go. But she wouldn't do that. Not to them.

"I need you guys to trust me. Please? I'll find you when I'm done, I promise."

Lewis and Bennett were quiet for a long moment before they nodded reluctantly. Neither of them asked what she was doing or *still* had to do. Whatever it was, she was entitled to it. They knew that.

Dr. Waters, Lewis, and Bennett were almost back at the stairwell door when Jade spoke again.

"Dr. Waters?" she called. The woman stopped, turned. "What floor?"

Lewis and Bennett were confused by the question, but Ruth Waters was not.

"Ten," she answered.

Jade nodded, and just as they were about to leave again, she spoke one more time. "Dr. Waters." The woman turned again. The air suddenly had that strange buzz to it. "You keep them safe."

A shiver ran down the doctor's spine. Despite the literal vibration in the air, she could feel the danger that would come her way if she disobeyed that command. But she couldn't help but feel a little proud of Jade. She had finally found something that she cared for, that she *loved*, and she was trying to protect it. Dr. Waters nodded her head. “I will. I swear it.”

III

There were thirty men stationed along the hall that led to Thomas O'Riley's office. He had commanded them to stay after the announcements had started.

Thomas had seen the entire encounter in Jade's room with Dr. Peters and what had happened in the hall immediately after, before he turned off the system in a panic. He grabbed his gun from a drawer in his desk and placed it in easy reach on the flat surface before he started pacing the floor.

"What the fuck am I supposed to do?" he muttered to himself as he walked back and forth, back and forth across the carpet. His heart was hammering in his chest, and he was starting to get a headache. All his desire to be in the field, seeing the action and being in the middle of it all, was leaving him. He felt like maybe he really was designed to sit back and watch it all happen. Sitting back behind that window, out of sight, while he watched Dr. Peters do his work: it had been much more fulfilling than he'd thought it was going to be. "I wasn't trained for this shit!" He stopped suddenly, silent, listening for any indication that someone outside might have heard him. After a few moments passed and nothing happened, he started pacing again. Back and forth, back and forth.

Jade had ascended five flights of stairs by the time Thomas decided he could no longer sit in his office and wait. He needed to get out of there, needed to take his chances of getting out of the building alive. He grabbed his gun and hurriedly walked to the office door but stopped suddenly as his hand closed around the door-knob.

You're making a mistake, a small voice said from the deep dark corners of his mind. His brows furrowed and his grip on the knob loosened. He hesitated for a moment before becoming angry. He bared his teeth, turned the knob, and threw the door open. The men positioned outside didn't say a word as Thomas started storming down the hall. As he passed, they fell into line behind, beside, and in front of him.

The hairs on the backs of their necks and arms stood on end. The air felt like at any moment it could start jostling them around. The florescent lights above them flickered for a brief second.

At the far end of the hall, almost in slow motion, the unmistakable form of Jade turned the corner. Thomas's heart felt like it stopped. He stopped walking, but the men around him did not. As they spotted her, they raised their weapons. All the sound abruptly muffled for Thomas, and there was a ringing in his ears. Everything had slowed.

He watched as Jade started making her way down the hall. He watched as the armed men started shouting for her to stop. He was paralyzed with fear. The lights above flickered again, and the first gunshot rang out in a muffled explosion of sound. It made Thomas jump. Jade kept walking.

Soon, most of the men were firing as they pressed forward. Thomas did not move. His feet felt like lead, his legs like jelly. But this wasn't Jade's doing, and he knew that, which made him all the more frustrated and embarrassed.

Thomas watched as the bullets left the barrels of the guns they were fired from and started cutting through the air toward Jade. And he saw the exact moment—so quick that if he had blinked, he would have missed it—when the bullets stopped moving two inches from Jade's body, the directions reversed, and the bullets buried themselves deep into the skulls of the men who had fired them. All the while, Jade did not react. She kept walking as bodies were falling dead around her. Her eyes never left Thomas. The lights above her flickered as she passed them.

With shaky hands, Thomas raised his own gun. He was watching it all as if he were just a tiny man sitting inside of the head of another person, watching life through that person's eyeballs, like windows. He fired once, and the bullet flew, almost reaching her and then veering and striking the wall to her left at the last second. A pit formed in his stomach. He fired two more times, and the same thing happened with those bullets. He flinched as they each struck the wall.

Jade was halfway down the hall now and still steadily approaching. Thomas let his hands drop to his sides as he took a few stumbling steps backward. Gun still in hand, he turned and sprinted full speed back to his office. He threw the door open and slammed it shut behind him, aggressively turning the lock and throwing himself across the room. He tumbled until his back hit the front of his desk.

He was breathing quickly, staring at the door with wide eyes. His heart was still hammering in his chest, and he thought this must have been what Director Harris felt right before he had his heart attack and died. Thomas had wondered if his death was caused by the knowledge that Jade was returning to the facility. But now, he was certain of it. The panic he felt knowing that she was coming for him solidified that hypothesis in his mind as fact.

Thomas watched as the lock on the door started to move. It clicked, and he genuinely thought his bowels were going to loosen. In a scramble, he half-crawled, half-scurried around the desk and tried to fit himself into the hollow where his legs would go. His gun was still in his hand, and he held it tightly in his grip.

He squeezed his eyes shut and covered his mouth with his free hand, trying to quiet the sound of his raspy breathing. His eyes flew open at the slow creaking sound of the hinges as the door opened. He could feel her step into the room, but he could not hear any of her footsteps across the carpeted floor.

The air was vibrating, and his skin turned to goose flesh.

The thrum in the air intensified with every second that passed until his whole body felt like it was TV static. Then it stopped, and he felt nothing, and everything was silent. Thomas held his breath. He wanted to hold on to the hope that she had left. That she had just wanted to scare him. He shifted his position slightly, and the desk seemed to disappear in a blink. He heard it crash against the far wall before he saw it fall to the ground in pieces. And there she was, on the other side of the phantom desk, crouched down at his level, a foot away from him.

He shrieked and scrambled backward using his heels and his palms until his back hit the giant windows. She stayed like that, in the crouched position, for what felt like a lifetime, just looking at him.

Thomas's eyes were welling up with frightful tears. He felt lightheaded, like he could pass out at any second. Jade cocked her head slightly to one side before she plopped down and crisscrossed her legs so that she was now sitting in front of him. The sudden movement made him jump, and he tried scooting even closer to the window.

His mouth opened with the intention of saying something, but the words caught in his throat. Without thinking, he raised the gun to aim it at her. Before he could even squeeze the trigger, the gun crumpled in his hand like an aluminum can. He dropped it, defeated.

"Why—" His voice caught in his throat. He swallowed. "Why are you doing this?" Tears were falling down his face. "Why me?"

Jade didn't answer. She continued to look at him from where she sat, not moving. Thomas's eyes moved rapidly across her whole frame. He didn't want to look her in the face. He thought it would make it too real.

"You didn't bother putting this much effort into killing Dr. Peters," he continued. "And—" he cleared his throat. "And he was the one who made you like this."

She moved a little, causing him to finally bring his gaze to her face.

"No," she finally said. The sound of her voice made him feel like his skin was being poked with pins and needles. He felt like throwing up. "He didn't deserve my time."

A choked sob escaped his lips, and one of his hands flew up to cover the bottom of his face. A frown appeared on Jade's face.

"But you?" She scooted herself closer to him. She cocked her head to the side again. Her brows furrowed. "*You* were the one who brought me back here. And *you* were the one who broke a promise." Thomas's eyes went wide as he remembered. "You promised me that nothing would happen to Lewis and Bennett. And then you brought them *here*. To *the Lab*. I can't forgive you for that," she said, shaking her head from side to side.

"I was just doing my job," he whispered. He knew that he had gotten carried away in all this. He knew that he should have declined Dr. Peters's offer when it was presented to him that night in his motel room. But it had all seemed too *good*. It had given him an opportunity to take his revenge against Jade for the murder of his partner, James. And for a man like Thomas O'Riley, all that power was too important to pass up.

Jade nodded slightly. "I understand that," she said, her face shifting seamlessly to an expression of acceptance. But then it switched again, and her face was dark. Angry. *Vengeful*. "Now I need you to understand that this is mine."

Thomas let out a heavy, shaky sigh and squeezed his eyes shut. Tears continued to slip down his face as Jade rose to her feet. She took a small step backward and watched him for a moment.

With a slight flex of Jade's hand, all the bones in Thomas's body started breaking, beginning at his feet and ending with both clavicles. His broken ribs punctured his lungs, and he could feel the strange sensation of them starting to fill with blood. He opened his mouth to scream, and, with force, his jaws slammed shut and he bit straight through his tongue.

That'll teach you to tell lies, Jade thought as the loose chunk of Thomas's tongue rolled down his front and landed with a very soft thud against his ruined gun. Blood leaked out from between his lips and drenched the front of his suit. His breathing was filled with gurgling sounds and popping blood bubbles.

Tears streamed down his face, and his eyes suddenly locked with hers. He couldn't tell, at first, whether he had decided to look at her or she had *made* him look.

It was only when he attempted to close his eyes that he found his eyelids unable to move. The resistance was like someone's fingers were holding them open.

After staring at each other for a long moment, Jade finally broke his neck, and he went limp against the window. A wheezing sigh was the last sound Thomas O'Riley ever made.

IV

Lewis, Bennett, and Dr. Waters stood five yards behind the tree line. They'd been watching the door to the stairwell exit intently for almost thirty minutes, and still no sign of Jade. Dr. Waters was sure that she would end up coming out the same way they had. The stairs were her only option of descent since the elevators weren't working.

There was a handful of other Lab workers who had also made their way outside, either because they were nervous about the announcements or because the people around them had been. None of them saw the trio where they stood.

Bennett had Lewis's left hand held tightly in his right as he watched the exit. He feared looking away and risking the possibility of missing her. Lewis was also watching the door, but his eyes would also often venture around to the sides of the building and the other people standing around. He didn't want them to be so focused on one place that they missed something else coming. He was absentmindedly biting the nails on his free hand as he did so.

Dr. Waters was watching the windows, looking for any signs that things might be escalating inside. She saw nothing but the occasional shadow of someone walking by.

The door leading to the stairwell suddenly opened, and they all held their breath. Then there she was, standing in the doorway. She did not see them where they hid. She *did* see the few Lab workers who were scattered around, but she paid them no mind. Bennett made a move like he was going to shout for her, but Dr. Waters stopped him.

"We can't give ourselves away yet."

Bennett was just about to ask why when the exit door opened again, and ten men with guns came barging out. They saw Jade immediately, and none of them hesitated to start firing their weapons.

"Get down!" Dr. Waters hissed as bullets started whizzing by into the trees. They all dropped to the floor, but not before a bullet caught Dr. Waters in the throat, sending her teetering backward. She landed on her back, and blood started gushing out of the fresh hole in her neck. She lay there for a long, agonizing moment, choking on her own blood, before letting out one last gurgling sigh, and there was nothing.

Lewis and Bennett were horrified as they lay huddled together on the ground beside her. Bennett had his arms up and around his and Lewis's heads as bullets continued to fly.

Jade was deflecting all the bullets that were fired her way. Some turned and struck the ground, and others hit the building or went into the trees. A few even struck and killed the other Lab workers who had left the building. After a few moments, the armed men started to fly in different directions, as if an invisible cane had reached out and yanked them away. Necks broke, spines snapped, or bullets hit warm bodies until Jade was the only one standing.

The silence that followed was almost peaceful. Bennett dared to lift his head just enough to see what was going on in front of them. It was like the scene from the hall where they found her on the fourth floor. Lumps of black and white cloth were littered across the grass, and Jade stood like a lone tree in the middle of an empty field. She turned in a slow circle, her eyes moving across the carnage around her. Bennett saw her shoulders starting to shake and knew that she had begun to cry.

She hadn't *wanted* so many people to die. She had only really wanted to be rid of Thomas and Dr. Peters. But there was always collateral damage in these kinds of things. She thought she could live with the reality of becoming a carnifex, but she didn't want to think about it *now*. She wasn't finished yet.

With the heels of her palms, she wiped her face roughly and looked up at the building beside her. Her eyes slowly moved up from floor to floor.

"Jade!"

The sudden sound almost made her jump out of her skin. She whipped around, the air beginning to buzz, and caught the standing figures of Lewis and Bennett just beyond the tree line with her eyes. Bennett was waving his arms above his head and lowered them once he was sure she'd seen them. They both took a few steps toward her before suddenly finding themselves unable to move. Jade was holding her hands up to communicate that they should stay there. The pressure on their bodies disappeared, and they quickly realized she had stopped them from walking. She held up one finger. *Wait a second*, it said. They nodded. What more she needed to do they couldn't possibly guess. But they trusted her, so they would wait.

They stayed in place as they watched her walk to the edge of the tree line and stop. She looked in at them and gave them an almost wary sort of smile before turning around to face the building again.

Jade took a deep breath and let it out slowly. She took another, and as she exhaled the air started to vibrate. Lewis and Bennett could have sworn they could feel it in the ground beneath their feet too.

Her right arm slowly began to rise above her head, and her fist closed as if she were grabbing hold of an invisible handle. Then her left arm rose and her hand grasped. Jade took another deep breath. She held it, and with a great yanking downward of her arms, the building began to crumble. From top to bottom, the floors started to fall in on each other. The ground beneath them started to shake and they all had trouble keeping their footing. Jade turned and started running into the trees.

"Come on!" she yelled over the thundering sounds of the building coming down right before their eyes. She grabbed hold of their wrists and started dragging them deeper into the woods.

They did not turn back until they reached the top of a hill about a mile north of the Lab. Jade dropped onto the grass and lay on her back, panting. Lewis and Bennett sat down on either side of her. After catching her breath, Jade sat up and looked in the direction of the building. Smoke was rising in thick, black plumes. The orange of the fire stood out brightly against the green of the trees and the darkening of the sky.

Lewis wrapped an arm around Jade, and Bennett wrapped one of his own around Lewis and Jade both. They sat like that, there on the hill, until the sky was completely dark. Jade watched with ineffable triumph as her old world burned before her very eyes. She sighed deeply and wedged herself closer into her new one.

The End

EPILOGUE

"Tell me again," Jade said, pulling her legs up onto the chair, a smile stretching across her face. "Tell me the story again."

Lewis and Bennett began to laugh from where they sat on the bench just across from her. The sky was painted orange and pink. The three of them sat out on the back porch of Bennett's mom's old house. They had bought it five years ago.

"Again?" Bennett chuckled. "But you ask for it every year!" A light blush crept to Jade's cheeks, and she shrugged her shoulders.

"Yeah, I know. I like hearing it," she smiled wide. "And besides, you can't deny me on my birthday."

Lewis grinned and leaned into Bennett's shoulder.

"You heard her," Lewis teased. "Go ahead and tell it."

Bennett rolled his eyes, opened his mouth to start telling the tale, and Jade stopped him.

"Wait!" she interrupted. "I want Lewis to tell it this time."

"Oh, this'll be good." Bennett laughed, draping an arm over Lewis's shoulders. Lewis tried to protest, and Jade gave him a frown.

"Come on, Lewis. Bennett always tells it. I want you to tell it this time."

"Can't deny her on her birthday," Bennett reminded him. Lewis looked up at him with an exasperated expression.

"Whose side are you on, anyway?"

"Please?" Jade said, giving him an exaggerated pout. Lewis sighed and nodded his head.

"Ok, ok, I'll tell it."

Jade clapped her hands and made herself into an even tighter ball in her chair.

"For the birthday girl herself: the story of how Bennett and I met," Lewis announced in a mock commercial voice, causing Jade to giggle. And he began telling the story.

Lewis sat in a janky fold-up chair by the fire pit, alone. In the net cup holder sat an untouched plastic cup filled with cheap beer. Behind him he could hear the muffled voices of people talking loudly over music that blared over huge speakers inside the house. There was a sudden explosion of triumphant voices from a group playing a drinking game.

Lewis didn't really like parties. He preferred more intimate gatherings, with a much smaller crowd. But it was his friend Alex's birthday, so he agreed to be uncomfortable for a few hours.

He shoved his hands into his jacket pockets and propped his feet up on the edge of the fire pit. Lewis could see his breath floating out in front of his face with every exhale. He finally picked up his cup and took a sip, making a face as he tasted and swallowed the alcohol. He was grateful for the tiny bit of warmth it would give him.

One of the back doors to the house opened, making the chaos inside that much louder, and closed again. Lewis listened as slightly sloppy footsteps walked across the backyard toward where he sat. He turned his head to look at the person walking up and gave him a smile.

"Hey, Alex," Lewis greeted him.

Alex grinned and raised the cup in his hand to Lewis. "Hey, buddy," he said, and he sat down in one of the other chairs around the fire. "You having a good time?"

"Eh," Lewis shrugged his shoulders. "I'm all right. You know big parties aren't really my thing."

Alex nodded and took a sip of his drink. He laughed a little. "Yeah, I know. I appreciate you coming over, though."

"Of course."

They sat quietly for a moment, each with his eyes glued to the flickering flames.

"You know, if you wanna get out of here, there's no hard feelings," Alex said, causing Lewis to look at him.

"Oh, Alex I—"

Alex put up a hand, cutting him off. "No, really," he said, and Lewis could tell he wasn't being condescending or negative in any way. "I know you don't like this kinda stuff. I just appreciate that you even showed up," he repeated. Lewis nodded. He really did want to go home, put on some comfy clothes, and get into bed. Whether or not he was going to read or watch TV was up to fate. He thought about it for a few moments.

"Ok," he finally said. "I'll stay for a few more minutes and then I guess I'm gonna head out."

Alex smiled at him and stood from his seat. He wavered a little but straightened himself out quickly. "Sounds good to me, buddy. I'm gonna go back inside, but you come and find me before you go, ok? Don't forget to say goodbye."

"I won't."

Alex patted Lewis on the shoulder as he passed him on his way back inside the house. He heard the back door open, letting out all the sound, and then the party was muffled again.

Lewis sighed and sank into his chair so that his head was level with the back of the chair. He leaned his head back and looked up at the clear sky above him. Clusters of stars twinkled brightly in the inky blackness. He could see the smoke from the fire rising to meet them. He sat that way for almost fifteen minutes before finally getting up, grabbing his cup, and heading back into the house.

The heat was drastically different from outside. The constant movement of bodies through the closed-up house made it feel like Lewis had just stepped into a sauna. And the music was so loud that he could barely hear himself think, let alone what anyone was saying.

Lewis tried his best to worm his way through the unforgiving sea of people, standing on his toes every so often, looking for Alex. He finally spotted his friend sitting on a couch with six other people. As Lewis took a step forward, the people directly to the right of him decided to suddenly turn around and walk straight into him. More than half of the drink in his hand now soaked through the front of his jacket. He could feel the cold already seeping into the fabric of the T-shirt he had on underneath.

The people who had run into him and caused the mess didn't seem to notice a thing and kept shoving their way on through. Lewis sighed deeply, growing more and more frustrated as time passed. Finally, he reached the couch where Alex was sitting.

"Lewis!"

He could barely hear Alex shout as he neared.

"Guys, this is Lewis!" Alex yelled at the people sitting around him.

They all waved, and some tried saying words to him, but he couldn't hear them and didn't really care.

"I'm gonna go ahead and go," Lewis shouted, pointing toward the front door with his thumb.

Alex's brows raised and his mouth dropped open to speak again. "Wait! I want you to meet everyone!"

Lewis could tell that Alex was starting to really get drunk, and he hoped his friends weren't as inebriated as he was. Otherwise, these introductions were going to take forever.

"Lewis this is…" But Lewis couldn't make out any of the names of any of the people until Alex got to the last one. "And this is Bennett!"

Bennett stood from where he was sitting—rather uncomfortably—on the arm of the couch. He gave Lewis a smile and a friendly wave.

"Hi," Bennett mouthed. Lewis couldn't help but smile back at him and gave a small wave in return.

"Are you enjoying the party?" Bennett asked, leaning closer to Lewis so he could hear. It was then that Lewis noticed that Alex and all the other people he had introduced had already gone back to whatever they were doing before he'd come over. And here Bennett was, talking to him.

"I was just about to leave, actually," Lewis answered. He was shoved forward suddenly by people passing behind him and was tossed into Bennett's side. Bennett grabbed him by his shoulders to steady him. Lewis could feel heat rushing to his face.

"I'm sorry."

"No, don't be, it wasn't your fault." Bennett's eyes scanned over the room for a moment before coming back to Lewis. He had a thoughtful sort of expression. "Do you wanna go outside?" he blurted out. "I'm sure it's not nearly as loud out there."

Lewis thought about it for a moment. He looked toward the front door, where he had been headed. But there was something about this guy. This *Bennett.* He looked back to the man in front of him and saw an almost pleading look on his face. Lewis nodded.

"There's a fire pit out back," he said and allowed himself to be led back in the direction he had just come from by this stranger.

"Ah, this is much better," Bennett said the moment they reached the outside and Lewis shut the back door behind them. They walked together, Lewis slightly behind Bennett, over to the fire pit and sat down next to each other in the janky chairs.

"So, how do you know Alex?" Lewis asked. He wasn't sure what else to say, but he'd found himself suddenly really wanting to talk to Bennett.

A nervous smile formed on Bennett's face, and he rubbed the back of his neck sheepishly.

"I don't, actually," he answered. "My friend Adam invited me sort of last minute, and I didn't have any other plans for tonight." He laughed a little. "I wasn't expecting there to be so many people, though. I'm much more into smaller crowds."

"You and me both," Lewis said with a smile. He shrugged his shoulders. "But that's Alex. His literal motto for life is 'go big or go home.'" Bennett laughed, and a nervous but also excited feeling bloomed in Lewis's stomach. He liked hearing Bennett laugh. He suddenly blushed at the thought and tried to shove it away.

A shiver ran through him, and he suddenly realized just how cold he was. He tried wrapping his arms around himself but that only made the wetness of his jacket soak more into his T-shirt. The sound of his teeth chattering made Bennett look over at him.

“Are you ok?” Bennett asked. There was genuine concern on his face and in his voice. Lewis nodded, but it looked a little more like a spasm than a nod since his whole body was now shivering.

“Yeah, I’m g-good,” Lewis answered through gritted teeth. “I just had my drink spilled on me a few minutes ago, so my jacket is just kinda soaked.”

“Well come on then,” Bennett said, standing from his chair. “I’ve got an extra jacket in my car.”

“No, it’s ok, you don’t have to—” But Bennett had already grabbed his hand and was leading him around the house toward the street where Bennett’s car was parked. He didn’t let go of Lewis’s hand until they had reached the vehicle and he started rummaging around in his back seat. He stood after a few moments with a dark gray crew-neck sweatshirt.

“Here, put this on.” Bennett said, handing it over to Lewis. Lewis hesitated for a second, then grabbed it with one shaky hand.

“Thank you.” Lewis said in a small voice as he took off his jacket, which Bennett took and held in his hands so that Lewis didn’t have to put it on the ground, and pulled the sweatshirt over his head. It was really baggy and really warm.

“Sorry it’s so huge,” Bennett said with a small smile. He had a nervous kind of energy about him, but it was also warm and kind. “I’m a total sucker for oversized sweatshirts.” Lewis laughed and Bennett handed him his jacket.

"I totally get it," Lewis chuckled. "It's like being wrapped in a big hug." And he wrapped his arms around himself dramatically and Bennett laughed again.

"Exactly!"

Lewis walked over to his car and threw his jacket onto the passenger seat, and then the two of them walked back around the house to sit by the fire again. The thought of leaving was no longer on Lewis's mind.

They sat and talked for almost three hours. They had started with the smaller, more trivial stuff, like What's your favorite color? (Lewis's is hunter green, and Bennett's is sky blue), What are your hobbies? (Lewis likes to read, and Bennett *loves* to sleep), What's your favorite holiday? (Lewis and Bennett both love Halloween and Thanksgiving), and so on.

Then they moved on to the deeper stuff, like What's your family like? (Bennett told him about his dad's death in a car accident shortly after he was born and how it was just him and his mom; Lewis said that his parents were nice and that he wasn't able to see them very often since moving away for school), What's your biggest fear? (Lewis said his was losing the people he loves, and Bennett said his was being alone—not physically, but mentally), Where do you see yourself in five years? (they agreed that looking too far into the future made them anxious because making plans or having ideas for themselves that they may not be able to fulfill made them feel unfairly disappointed).

They had just started talking about memories that stuck out to them as kids when the back door to the house opened and Bennett's friend Adam came out.

"I've been looking everywhere for you, man!" Adam said in a relieved tone as he walked across the grass toward where Lewis and Bennett were sitting. "Jamie's totally blacked out," he said with a light laugh as he reached them. "We should definitely get him back home."

Bennett's eyes immediately shifted from his friend over to Lewis. There was disappointment and a little bit of sadness on his face now. And it was obvious then that Bennett didn't want to go because he wanted to stay and keep talking to Lewis. It made that excited-nervous feeling appear again in Lewis's stomach. Bennett sighed and nodded his head reluctantly.

"Yeah, ok." And he stood from his chair slowly. Adam had already started back for the house by the time Bennett had stood fully. Bennett looked at Lewis, and he could tell that Bennett wanted to say something. It was also like he was stalling his departure.

"I'll walk you out," Lewis offered, and a smile crept onto Bennett's face, brightening it again. He nodded, and Lewis stood from his chair. As slowly as they could, they walked around the house quietly.

They were standing on the front lawn for a few minutes before Bennett's friends finally came out, two of them dragging who Lewis assumed to be Jamie, out of the house and over to Bennett's car. It was only when the small group had exited the house that Lewis realized that he and Bennett were standing so close to each other that their shoulders were mere centimeters away from touching. He took a very small step to the side, hoping Bennett wouldn't notice.

Bennett watched his friends as they struggled to get Jamie into the back seat for a few moments before turning to face Lewis.

"So, when can I see you again?" he asked and caught Lewis off guard.

"You want to see me again?" Lewis asked stupidly, and it made Bennett laugh.

"Well yeah," Bennett laughed. "I really liked talking to you." He shrugged his shoulders, a kind of joking energy building around him. "Besides, I'll have to get that sweatshirt back somehow," he teased. Lewis rolled his eyes and they both burst into laughter.

"Well, when are you free?" Lewis asked as the laughter subsided. Bennett thought for a moment, hesitated, and then asked:

"How about tomorrow?"

Lewis blushed, and he was thankful for how dark it was outside. He nodded his head.

"Yeah. Yeah, I can do tomorrow." A huge grin stretched across Bennett's face, and he shoved his hands into his pockets.

"Awesome. It's a date then."

"Bennett, come on!" Adam shouted from where he stood by the car. Bennett went to take a step and stopped suddenly.

"Wait! Give me your phone," he said, and Lewis dug in his pockets and handed it over. Bennett put in his number and sent a text. He handed the phone back.

"I'll call you tomorrow, ok?"

Lewis nodded.

"Ok."

Bennett turned and started walking to his car. He took a few steps before he stopped and turned back to Lewis.

"Bye," Bennett said.

"Bye," Lewis replied with a small wave. Then he watched as Bennett turned again, walked to his car, and drove away.

"And I've seen this dork almost every day since." Lewis finished the story. Bennett rolled his eyes and smiled.

"You know you love me," he teased, squeezing Lewis's shoulders.

"Yeah, I do."

Jade really did love that story. It always filled her with such a surplus of warmth and love and happiness, and she was grateful for it. It made her feel like all her past stuff was a little bit worth it if it meant she was able to be here now, with Lewis and Bennett, and feel this kind of happiness.

"All right," Bennett said, standing from the bench. By now, the sun had completely set, and the only light came from the two small porch lights on either side of the sliding glass door. "Time for cake!"

Lewis and Jade both rolled their eyes and laughed. Every year, Bennett made her a cake for her birthday, and every year he was the one most excited to eat it. Bennett offered Lewis his hand, which Lewis took, and the three of them went inside the house.

They had their cake, and they watched a movie, and then Jade went off to her room for the night.

"I love you guys," Jade said, like she did every night, before she entered the long hallway.

"We love you too," they both replied.

When she'd gone into her room and shut the door behind her, she walked over to the bedside table and opened one of the drawers. Inside was a small photo album. She sat down on her bed and started flipping through the pages.

Jade finally had her own pictures.

Milton Keynes UK
Ingram Content Group UK Ltd.
UKHW010832190424
441445UK00004B/144